id Ga'
A R
ion and

ou

**"Instinctively, I Want To Kiss You. But I've Had That Particular Instinct For A Long Time Now, And I'm Not Sure I Should Trust It."**

Danielle smiled. "You should trust it."

His hands moved to her face, cradling it gently in his palms. "What about my other instincts?"

"You have other instincts?"

"To toss you down on the grass and ravish you in the moonlight."

Want and need instantly cascaded through her, robbing her of her breath. She wished it didn't sound so tempting. There were a million complicated reasons to keep her distance from Travis, even if her own desires were screaming at her to ignore them.

She came up on her toes to meet him. "Let's take it one instinct at a time."

# The Last Cowboy Standing

## BARBARA DUNLOP

MILLS & BOON®

First published in Great Britain 2014
by Mills & Boon, an imprint of Harlequin (UK) Limited,
Large Print edition 2014
Eton House, 18-24 Paradise Road,
Richmond, Surrey, TW9 1SR

© 2014 Barbara Dunlop

ISBN: 978 0 263 24429 8

Harlequin (UK) Limited's policy is to use papers that are natural, renewable and recyclable products and made from wood grown in sustainable forests. The logging and manufacturing processes conform to the legal environmental regulations of the country of origin.

Printed and bound in Great Britain
by CPI Antony Rowe, Chippenham, Wiltshire

## BARBARA DUNLOP

writes romantic stories while curled up in a log cabin in Canada's far north, where bears outnumber people and it snows six months of the year. Fortunately she has a brawny husband and two teenage children to haul firewood and clear the driveway while she sips cocoa and muses about her upcoming chapters. Barbara loves to hear from readers. You can contact her through her website, www.barbaradunlop.com

To my mother, with love.

# One

Travis Jacobs could do anything for eight seconds. At least, that's what he told himself every time he climbed up the side of a bull chute. Tonight's Vegas crowd was loud and enthusiastic, their attention centered on the current rider being bucked around the arena by Devil's Draw.

Putting the other cowboys in the competition from his mind, he looked at Esquire below him, checking for any sign of agitation. Then he rolled his cuffs up a couple of turns, pulled his brown Stetson low and tugged a worn, leather glove onto his right hand.

The crowd groaned in sympathy a mere second before the horn sounded, telling Travis that Buckwheat Dawson had come off the bull. Up next, Travis swung his leg over the chute rail and drew a bracing breath. While Karl Schmitty held the rope, he adjusted the rigging and wrapped his hand. Wasting no time, he slid up square on the bull and gave a sharp nod to the gate operator.

The chute opened, and all four of Esquire's feet instantly left the ground. The Brahma shot out into the arena then straight up in the air under the bright lights. The crowd roared its pleasure as the black bull twisted left, hind feet reaching high, while Travis leaned back, spurred, his arm up, muscles pumped, fighting for all he was worth to keep himself square on the animal's back.

Esquire turned right, twisting beneath Travis, shaking him as if he was a bothersome gnat. Three seconds turned to four. Travis's hand burned against the rope, and his wrist felt like it was about to dislocate. The strain sent a branching iron along his spine, but he also felt completely and totally alive. For a brief space of time, life was reduced to its essence. Nothing mattered but the battle between Travis and the bull.

Esquire made an abrupt left turn, nearly unseating Travis, but he kept his form. His hat flew off into the dust. The blaring music and the roar of the crowd disappeared, obliterated by the pulse of blood pumping past his ears.

The horn sounded just before Esquire made one final leap, unseating Travis, sending him catapulting through the air. Travis summersaulted, grazing the bull's left horn, quickly twisting his body to avoid hitting the ground head-on. His shoulder came down first, with his back taking the brunt of the impact. As the air whooshed out of his lungs, a face in the crowd danced before his eyes.

Danielle? What the heck was Danielle doing in Vegas?

Then Esquire's menacing form filled his vision, and he leaped to his feet. Corey Samson, one of the bullfighters, jumped between them, distracting the animal while Travis sprinted to the fence.

Glancing back, he realized Danielle had to be a figment of his imagination. The crowd was nowhere near close enough for him to recognize a particular face. He heaved himself over the top of the fence and jumped to the ground on the other side.

"Nice one." Buckwheat clapped him good-naturedly on the back.

"Hey, Travis," Corey yelled from inside the arena.

Travis turned to see Corey toss him his hat. He caught the Stetson in midair, and Corey gave him a thumbs-up.

"Ninety-one point three," the announcer cried into the sound system.

The crowd roared louder, while lasers and colored spotlights circled the arena, the music coming up once more. Travis was the night's last rider, meaning he'd just won ten thousand dollars.

He stuffed his hat on his head and vaulted back over the fence onto the thick dirt, waving to the crowd and accepting the congratulations of the clowns and cowboys.

"You have *got* to go pro," Corey shouted in his ear.

"Just blowin' off some steam," Travis responded, keeping his grin firmly in place for the spectators, knowing he'd be projected onto the Jumbotron.

His older brother, Seth, had recently been married, and he'd committed his next three years to working on the Lyndon Valley railway project. Responsibility for the family's Colorado cattle ranch now rested completely on Travis's shoulders. Faced with that looming reality, he'd discovered he had a few wild oats left to sow.

"You could make a lot of money on the circuit," said Corey.

Travis let himself fantasize for a minute about going on the road as a professional bull rider. The image was tantalizing—to be footloose and fancy free, no cattle to tend, no ranch hands, no bills, no responsibilities. He'd ride a couple of times a week, hit the clubs, meet friendly women. There were no bleak, dusty, hick towns on this particular rodeo circuit. It was all bright lights and five-star hotels.

For a moment, he resented the lost opportunity. But he forcibly swallowed his own frustration. If he'd wanted to be a bull rider, he should have spoken up before now. While his brother and sisters were all choosing their own life paths, Travis should have said something about leaving the ranch. But it was too late. He was the last Jacobs cowboy, and somebody had to run the place.

A small crowd had gathered in the middle of the arena to celebrate his win. He unzipped his flak jacket to circulate a little air. Then he accepted the prize buckle and the check from the event manager and gave a final wave of his hat to the crowd.

Mind still mulling what might have been, he turned and fell into step beside Corey, their boots puffing up dust as they moved toward the gate.

"How long have you been on the road?" he found himself asking the bullfighter.

"Nearly ten years now," Corey responded. "Started when I was seventeen."

"You ever get tired of it?"

"What's to get tired? The excitement? The adventure? The women?"

Travis stuffed the check in his shirt pocket. "You know what I mean."

"Yeah, I know. When I get tired of the wheels turning, I go back to the folks' place in New Mexico for a while."

"Ever tempted to stay there?" Travis was trying to reassure himself that life on the road got old, that all men eventually wanted a real home.

Corey shook his head. "Nope. Though, last trip home, there was this pretty red-haired gal living down the road."

Travis chuckled at the yearning expression on Corey's face. "I take it she's calling you back to New Mexico?"

"Not yet, but likely soon. She's got some kind of a bullfighter fantasy going on inside that head of hers, and she's decided I'm the fire she wants to play with."

Travis burst out laughing.

Corey grinned and cocked an eyebrow.

"No pretty women calling me back to my hometown." There was nothing calling to Travis except cattle and horses.

Though, for some reason, his thoughts moved back to Danielle. But she wasn't from his hometown, and she sure wasn't any young innocent. She was twenty-eight, only a year younger than Travis. She was a graduate of Harvard Law, a practicing lawyer and probably the smartest, most sophisticated woman he'd ever met. She also flat out refused to give him the time of day.

"Think of that as another reason to go on the road," Corey countered.

"I'm on the road right now," said Travis. There wasn't a reason in the world he couldn't be footloose for the next few days. He'd earned it, and he had a check in his pocket just itching to get spent.

"That you are." Corey clapped him on the back. "Let's hit the clubs and show off that new buckle of yours. I bet there are dozens of gorgeous ladies out there just dying to hear how you rode the bull a full eight seconds, and how I saved your life in the arena."

"Is that how you're going to play it? That you saved my life?"

"Damn straight," said Corey.

There were two men in the world Danielle Marin wanted to avoid. Unfortunately, both of them had turned up in Vegas.

She was attending an international law conference, so she'd been on alert for Randal Kleinfeld. It seemed likely the wunderkind D.C. attorney would show up for a lecture by his university mentor Stan Sterling. But Travis Jacobs had come out of left field, literally.

She'd been blindsided when the announcer called his name at the bull riding show, then mesmerized when the bucking bull burst from the chute. Travis made it look effortless, as if he'd been born on the back of a Brahma. That he'd won should have come as no surprise to her. When it came to all things ranching and rough stock, Travis was a master. Stone-faced and rugged, tough and no-nonsense, he was the absolute antithesis of the smooth-talking, urbane Randal.

Show over, and back at the conference hotel with her friends, Danielle couldn't help but ponder the differences between the two men. Travis sticking in her mind, she took a bracing swallow of her vodka martini.

"That's the spirit, Dani," called Astra Lindy from across the table, raising her cosmo in a mock toast.

"I told you it would be fun," said Nadine Beckman as she accepted a frozen Bellini from their waitress.

The four women were less than a mile from the bull riding arena, relaxing in the lobby lounge. The temperature was mid-seventies, a light breeze blowing in from the hotel pool and the gardens.

"It was a blast," Odette Gray agreed with an enthusiastic nod. "Cowboys have the sexiest butts." She'd gone with a light beer.

The other two women laughed. Danielle smiled, keeping her expression lighthearted, even as she called up a mental image of Travis walking away. It simply wasn't fair. How could so much sexiness be wrapped up in such an exasperating man? And what kind of character flaw made her want him?

She took another healthy sip of her drink, regretting that she'd let her three friends talk her into the bull riding excursion. It had seemed like a harmless diversion after a full day of conference topics like Comparative Legal Systems and Cross Border Taxation. And it should have been a harmless diversion. Who could have predicted that Travis Jacobs would choose this week to leave Lyndon Valley and show up in Vegas?

"I'd do a cowboy," Nadine brazenly declared.

"In a heartbeat," Odette agreed.

"Up close, they're dusty and crude," Danielle pointed out, speaking to herself as much as to the other women. "They talk slow, use short sentences, very small words."

"Crude can be sexy," said Nadine. "And the dust washes off."

Sadly, deep down in her secret heart of hearts, Danielle agreed. She'd once seen Travis after he'd cleaned up. The result had made her gasp for breath, and put her libido into overdrive.

"Dani knows cowboys," said Astra. "She spends a lot of time in Colorado."

"I wouldn't call it a *lot* of time," Danielle corrected.

Truth was, she avoided Lyndon Valley as much as possible. The Jacobs spread was right next to the Terrell ranch. And Caleb Terrell was one of her major clients. He lived in Lyndon Valley only part-time, so she could usually arrange to put in her hours for Active Equipment at his Chicago head office or at her own law office on the Chicago River.

"Caleb's a cowboy," said Astra. "He doesn't use small words."

"I was generalizing," Danielle admitted.

On a night like tonight, she needed to take every opportunity to remind herself there was a world of difference between her and Travis Jacobs. She was closer to Randal in background, values, temperament and, of course, profession.

She'd dated Randal in law school, breaking up with him at graduation when he secured a prime internship in D.C. and she had accepted the offer in Chicago. He'd wanted to stay together, but she knew it wouldn't work out. Long-distance relationships never did. Plus, she hadn't been convinced he was *the one*. He was close, and she couldn't exactly say what was missing. But her instincts had told her to end it.

Randal had not been happy with the split. Not that he had anything to complain about the way things turned out. He was rising fast on the D.C. legal scene. The firm he worked for, Nester and Hedley, had clients that included senators, congressmen and captains of international industry. Danielle's Chicago job was bush-league by comparison.

Which made it strange that a partner from Nester and Hedley had contacted her last week, making her an offer that was all but impossible to refuse. She could only assume Randal had a hand in it, and she didn't know whether to thank him or berate him.

The job would give her a chance to build toward an equity partnership in a prestigious, cutting-edge firm. Any lawyer would jump at that. But she didn't want to be beholden to Randal. And she didn't want to date him again. Maybe she was being ridiculously conceited, but she couldn't help but wonder if that would turn out to be part of the package.

"Good evening, ladies," drawled a male voice.

She glanced up to see a vaguely familiar man in a black cowboy hat, a blue-and-green Western shirt and faded blue jeans. A split second later, she caught sight of Travis slightly behind him, worn Stetson low on his brow, face tanned brown, a challenging glint in his cobalt eyes.

She was honestly too tired for this.

"Are you from the rodeo?" asked Nadine, glancing from one to the other.

"We are," the stranger answered.

Astra pointed to Travis. "He's the guy who won, isn't he?"

"Are you a bull rider, too?" Nadine chirped to the other man.

"I'm a bullfighter."

"So, one of the clowns?" she asked.

"There's a big difference between a clown and a bullfighter, ma'am. For example." He jabbed this thumb toward Travis. "I saved this guy's life tonight."

"I saw that," Odette put in knowingly.

"Nice buckle." Nadine had turned her attention and her brilliant smile to Travis. She reached out and touched the shiny, gold and silver prize at his waist.

Danielle couldn't help but roll her eyes at the bling. Really? He had to wear it?

"This is Travis Jacobs," the stranger introduced, removing his hat. "He's tonight's bull riding champion. And I'm Corey Samson, bullfighter extraordinaire."

"Did he really save your life?" Odette asked Travis on a note of awe. Danielle knew the question was more about flirting than any true amazement at Corey's feat.

Corey looked to Travis and waited.

"He most certainly did," Travis acknowledged staunchly. "Bullfighters are highly skilled, highly trained, and among the bravest men on the planet."

The word *wingman* flitted through Danielle's brain. Travis was trying to help his friend pick up Odette.

Nadine turned to her. "That wasn't short sentences and small words."

Travis's challenging gaze turned on Danielle. It was clear he remembered her using that particular phrase in the past.

"It was a generalization," she repeated, refusing to break eye contact with him.

"That's very impressive," Odette told Corey with an almost comical flutter of her eyelashes.

"Danielle is continuously unequivocal in her elevated specifications for interactive discourse," said Travis, keeping his expression completely neutral.

"How does he know your name?" Astrid immediately demanded.

"We met in Colorado," said Travis.

"Briefly," Danielle pointed out.

"Dance?" Corey asked Odette.

"Love to." She giggled as she came to her feet.

"Dance?" Travis asked Danielle.

"Too busy with my drink," she responded airily, lifting her long-stemmed glass.

"I'll dance with you," Nadine chimed in with obvious enthusiasm, holding out a hand.

"Ma'am," Travis answered her, gallantly tipping his hat, taking her hand and helping her to her feet.

"You know a real live bull riding champion?" Astrid asked Danielle as the two couples left the covered deck for the dance floor inside, and Danielle concentrated on *not* looking at Travis's rear end.

"He's not a champion." Danielle went ahead and finished off the martini. "He only does it as a hobby."

"He's pretty good."

"That's what happens when you spend your entire life on a ranch in Lyndon Valley."

Astrid seemed confused by Danielle's tone. "You hold that against him?"

"What I hold against him is that he's annoying and incredibly full of himself. To hear him talk, differentiating between a Hereford and a Black Angus is the only knowledge relevant to mankind."

Astrid was obviously fighting a grin. "Did you mix the two up?"

Danielle sighed. "They do look a lot alike."

Astrid chuckled.

"He mocks me," Danielle elaborated. "All the time, on every level. And we only ever see each other at the ranch, so I'm always out of my element, and he has the advantage."

"You're a Harvard graduate."

"I *know.*"

"You shouldn't let him get to you."

"I don't."

"I can tell."

Danielle regrouped. "It's just that his frame of reference is so different than mine."

"And that ticks you off."

"What ticks me off, is that he's such a snob about it. I'm intelligent. I'm hard-working. People respect me, even other cowboys. Caleb and Reed are perfectly fine with me."

Astrid nodded toward the dance floor. "Looks like he's getting along fine with Nadine."

Danielle couldn't help a reflexive glance at the

couple as they danced together. "Nadine has probably been blinded by the shine off that enormous belt buckle."

"She always was attracted to winners."

Danielle couldn't help but take note of Travis's hand on the small of Nadine's back, her touch on his shoulder, the animated smile on his face, and the way she was chattering on to him. He twirled her around, and she laughed as he pulled her back, holding her even closer against him as they swayed to the music.

Danielle couldn't seem to stop a reflexive shimmer of sexual awareness from flashing through her belly. She pictured herself dancing with Travis. Then abruptly shook the image away.

"What's that?" asked Astrid.

"What?"

"You're blushing," Astrid accused.

"I am not."

"You got the hots for the bull rider."

"Not even a little bit."

"I think a little bit. I think more than a little bit."

"I'm ignoring it," Danielle declared, lifting her martini glass only to find it empty. She glanced around for the waitress. "I'm using intellect and reason to counteract inappropriate infatuation."

"You should dance with him," said Astrid.

"Not on your life."

"What happens in Vegas stays in Vegas."

"I'm sure not doing anything tonight that I have to leave in Vegas."

"I'm talking about dancing. What is it you have in mind?"

"Absolutely nothing."

She and Travis had come close to…well, close to *something* a couple of years back when he'd rescued her from a derelict barn. He'd mostly been amused, and she'd mostly been angry. But after they got back to his ranch house, and she'd showered and borrowed one of his sister's robes, there'd been a moment, a very long moment, when he'd look like he wanted to kiss her.

Her desire for that kiss had been so strong that it frightened her. She'd reacted defensively, uttering some patently untrue and hurtful remark. It had worked. He'd backed off. But it had also made him angry, and their relationship had never recovered.

"I see your drink is empty," Travis couldn't help saying to Danielle as he escorted Nadine to their table. He raised his brow in a question.

"That's your cue to dance with him." The woman called Astrid nudged Danielle with her elbow.

It was her cue to dance with him. Although he

fully expected her to shoot him down, he had to take the chance. Danielle was in front of him, and he wanted to touch her. It was as simple as that.

Nadine dropped into her chair at the table, crossing her shapely legs and taking a drink of something frozen and orange. "Go for it, Danielle," she breathed. "The band's great."

Danielle shook her head. "I'm not—" But then she stopped. Her eyes went wide, and she focused on a spot behind his shoulder. "Sure." She rose to her feet. "Why not?"

Travis glanced behind him, finding a smartly dressed man in his late twenties. He was clean-shaven. His light brown hair was slicked back, slightly shiny, neat around the ears. He wore an expensive, pin-striped suit, with a white dress shirt and a purple tie. The handkerchief in his pocket matched the tie, and his gaze was intent on Danielle.

"Dani," he opened with a dazzling, white smile.

"Sorry, Randal," she spoke breezily, linking her arm with Travis's. "Just about to dance." She all but dragged Travis toward the dance floor.

"What was that?" Travis asked, as he turned her into his arms.

"What was what?" she asked, all wide-eyed innocence.

"What was up with the guy back there?" He settled a hand on the small of her back.

"Nothing." She took a breath, placed her hand on his shoulder and stepped into the smooth jazz music.

She felt so good in his arms that he almost let her get away with it. The dance floor was crowded. The breeze from the open window ruffled her hair. Man, she was beautiful.

But he was too curious to let it drop. "You were about to turn me down. Don't pretend you weren't. Then that guy showed up, and you changed your mind."

Danielle gave her short, brown hair a little toss. It was soft and trendy, long across her eyes, wispy at her neck. "I didn't expect to see you in Vegas."

The longer he held her in his arms, the less he cared about the other guy. "Is that your way of telling me he's none of my business?"

"He *is* none of your business. But that's my way of telling you I don't want to talk about him."

"Okay by me."

"Thank you." There was an edge of sarcasm to her voice.

Travis was used to that. "I didn't expect to see you in Vegas, either."

"I'm attending an international law conference."

"Interesting?"

"It is if you like international law."

"Not exactly my forte."

"That's true, isn't it?"

"Why are you smiling?"

"Because, you're in my world now, cowboy."

He didn't exactly know what she meant by that. But he wasn't sure he wanted to pursue it, either, since it would likely mean they'd end up arguing. The way he saw it, Vegas was as much his world as hers.

"You saw me ride?" he asked instead.

"The girls dragged me along." She paused. "Bull riding is not exactly my sport of choice."

He wasn't about to take offense. He'd have been shocked speechless if she'd confessed to a secret love of bull riding. "Where were you sitting?"

She pulled back to look at him, her gaze quizzical. "Why?"

He wanted to know if he could have possibly seen her after his fall, but he wasn't about to explain that to her. "I wondered if you had a good view."

"Fourth row, across from the chutes."

"Good seats." He could have glimpsed her on the way down, maybe filed her image away in his subconscious and brought it up when he hit the dirt. It was possible.

She frowned. "I'm not sure being closer makes it any better."

"Are you trying to pick a fight?"

She hesitated almost imperceptibly. "We never seem to have to try."

Travis's skin prickled in warning, and he glanced around the room, catching the glare of the man who'd approached Danielle at the table. "Who *is* that guy?"

"I thought we'd moved on."

They might have moved on, but the other man obviously hadn't.

"Are you dating him or something?" Travis asked.

"No."

"No to dating him, or no to *or something.*"

She drew her arms from him. "This was a bad idea. I'm going back to the table now."

"He's waiting for you."

She reflexively turned her head, but Travis stopped her with a gentle palm on her cheek. "Don't look."

She stilled.

"He's staring daggers into me. If I'm gonna have to fight, you'd better warn me now."

She gave a weary smile and a small shake of her head. "Nobody's fighting."

Travis gathered her back into his arms, and she

picked up the rhythm again. His body gave a sub-conscious sigh, and he drew her closer this time, her chest brushing his, thighs meeting as they moved. She was exactly the right size, exactly the right shape. She fit perfectly into his arms.

"I'm pretty sure I can take him," he mused, breathing in the fresh fragrance of her hair.

"His name is Randal Kleinfeld. I knew him in law school."

"In the biblical sense?"

She tipped her head back, dark eyes chastising him. "You are insufferably rude, you know that?"

Travis might be rude, but Randal was intensely possessive. Not that Travis blamed him. Even he could see that Danielle was a gem, a beautiful, sen-suous, fiery gem of a woman. And for the right man, there'd be no looking back.

"Did you date him, Danielle?"

"It's business, Travis. He wants to talk to me about a job. With his firm. They've made me an offer to move to D.C."

Travis didn't like the sound of that. If she switched firms, she would also switch clients. She might never come back to Lyndon Valley on business with Caleb.

He tried to tell himself it didn't matter. They'd seen each other maybe a dozen times in the past two years. They were barely acquaintances. Mostly they fought. There was certainly nothing personal between them

Still, he found himself bracing for her answer as he posed the question. "Are you going to take it?"

"I don't know. That's why I don't want to talk to him. I don't need any pressure while I make up my mind."

Travis glanced at Randal again, taking in his clenched fists and the dark scowl that furrowed his aristocratic brow. It was patently obvious that he was after more than just a business relationship with Danielle. And Travis realized he had no way to stop him.

Not that he wanted to stop him. Danielle's personal life, in D.C. or anywhere else, was none of his business. He hoped it wasn't Randal's business. He hadn't seen much of the guy, but what he'd seen, he didn't like.

Thankfully Randal didn't have the upper hand, at least not at the moment anyway. Right now, Travis was the guy who had her in his arms, while Randal was the guy on the sidelines. He deliberately eased their bodies farther away from the crowd and splayed his hand across the small of her back, thinking he liked it this way.

# Two

The next morning, Danielle told herself that Travis's dancing her to the exit and spiriting her to the hotel elevator to get her away from Randal was no big deal. She didn't owe him any grand thank-you. She'd expressed her appreciation last night, and he'd been polite about it. It was done, over. It had accomplished its objective.

She didn't need to contact him again. In fact, it was better if she didn't contact him again. Their dancing last night had confirmed her secret fear. His body was as fit, as rock-hard and as sinewy as she'd fantasized.

He was tall and broad. His chin was square, nose just imperfect enough to be masculine. His blue eyes sparkled with what she swore had to be hidden secrets. And even fresh out of the bull riding arena, he smelled fantastic. She supposed he'd probably showered. But it wasn't any shampoo or cologne she'd reacted to last night. It was pure, male pheromones that had pushed up her pulse and made her skin tingle in anticipation of his touch.

When he'd pressed their bodies together, a rush of pure arousal had flooded her system. Through the back of her thin, satin tank top, she'd felt the individual calluses on his fingertips. Her breasts had brushed his denim shirt, teasing her nipples, making them embarrassingly hard. Under her own hands, she'd felt the solid strength of his shoulders, the shift of his muscles, and she'd longed to touch every inch of him.

Dancing with Travis was like secretly watching an erotic movie, or spending a week's pay at the spa or eating chocolate cupcakes with gobs of buttercream icing. You knew you shouldn't, but sometimes a woman couldn't help herself.

Now, she made her way to the Sinatra Room to attend a panel on emerging market tariff relief. There was a refreshment stand in the south lobby, and she'd left herself time to pick up a cup of coffee and a muffin. She was thankful that she'd stopped after one martini last night. For a few minutes there, she'd been tempted to order another.

"There you are, Dani," came Randal's friendly voice. "I don't know how I missed you last night."

"Good morning, Randal." She quickened her pace.

"Are you going to the tariff panel?"

She was tempted to say no so he wouldn't join her. But it was an important panel. And if he saw her there later, it would just be embarrassing.

"I am," she answered. "Just got to grab a coffee first." She veered off to the right.

"Coffee sounds great." He kept pace. "I'll buy. So, how've you been? How are things in Chicago?"

"Good," Danielle replied. "Business is brisk."

"You got the letter from Nester and Hedley?"

"I did."

They joined the long line snaking out of the small coffee shop.

"Nice offer?" he pressed.

"Did you have something to do with that?"

Randal held up his palms in a gesture of innocence. "I wish I had that kind of clout."

She checked his expression, not sure whether she was buying it or not. "You didn't bring me to the partners' attention?"

"I did not. I think they were impressed by the Schneider Pistole merger."

Danielle still wasn't convinced. "And how did they know about Schneider and Pistole?"

"Everybody knows about Schneider and Pistole. You successfully navigated some very protectionist waters. Bookmakers were giving it seven to one against."

"Very funny."

The line moved ahead, and they squeezed to one side to let departing patrons get past. The aromas of icing and cinnamon teased Danielle's senses. She'd told herself to go with a whole grain, fruit muffin. But the sweet confection was tempting.

Randal's attention went to the menu board near the ceiling. "I was saying to Laura just last week—"

"Is Laura one of the partners?" Danielle found it hard to believe he'd had nothing to do with the offer.

"Laura's my girlfriend."

"You have a girlfriend?"

"Don't sound so surprised."

"I thought…I mean…" Danielle didn't quite know where to go with this. She'd assumed he wanted to rekindle things with her. Had her ego led her that far astray?

"I'm a young, decently intelligent, decently looking man with a bright professional future."

"Of course you are." But the declaration sounded artificial even to her own ears.

Randal chuckled. "You should come to D.C., Danielle. It's where all the action is."

"There's a lot going on in Chicago, too."

They came to the counter.

"Why do I get the feeling you've maxed out there?" He looked to the clerk. "Two large coffees, one with cream and sugar, one black." Then he raised his brow to Danielle. "That still right?"

She nodded. She still sweetened and softened her coffee.

"I'll take a blueberry bran muffin," she told the young woman.

"Same for me," said Randal, reaching for his wallet.

"You don't have to buy."

"You wouldn't say that if you saw the number of zeros on my bonus check."

The clerk grinned brightly at his joke as she rang in their order, obviously aware that she was serving a good-looking, successful guy.

"That explains the Fendi suit," said Danielle.

"Come and work with me. The salary they quoted is only the beginning."

"I'm thinking about it," she admitted, accepting

one of the cardboard cups, and balancing the muffin in her other hand.

"Good." His smile went wide.

There was a momentary, overly friendly glint in his eye that gave her pause. But she quickly squelched her suspicion. The man had a girlfriend. The idea that he was still pining over her after all these years was ridiculous.

Still, as they started to walk away, he touched her elbow, and something familiar moved up her spine. She shook off the ridiculous reaction, stepping to one side. It was over between them. He had another girlfriend. And she was absolutely *not* one of those women who took another look at her ex as soon as he was taken by somebody else.

She took a nibble of the dense, molasses-based muffin as she navigated her way through the milling crowd. As she moved into the big lobby, a movement flashed at the corner of her eye. She turned her head and scanned the cavernous space. Suddenly, her gaze caught and held, a sensual awareness washing through her in earnest.

She swallowed.

Travis was leaning indolently against a marble pillar. He should have looked out of place in a plaid Western shirt and faded blue jeans amidst a sea of dark, designer suits, but he didn't. Somehow, the lawyers looked out of place around him.

"How's the muffin?" asked Randal, his voice startling her.

"Mmm. Good." She gave an appreciative nod.

Randal glanced at his watch, making a right turn toward the meeting room. "We'd better hurry."

"I guess." She wondered why Travis was here so early in the morning. In fact, why was he here at all? Last night, he'd told her he was staying at the Blonde Desert just off the Strip.

She half expected him to approach them. But he didn't. Just stood here, watching, a half smile on his face.

"Dani?" Randal prompted, stopping a half step ahead.

For some reason his voice was starting to grate.

"I'm coming," she answered, peering at Travis a moment longer.

Then she determinedly went ahead, setting a course for the panel discussion, determined to ignore Travis's presence, but fully aware of his form in her peripheral vision.

She wondered if he had a cell phone. If she knew the number, she could send him a text and ask him what he was doing in the hotel. It occurred to her that Caleb likely knew. She could text Caleb and ask him for Travis's cell. Would that be weird?

"Over there," said Randal, as they moved with the flow of the crowd through a set of double doors.

Astrid was waving at them from a classroom style table, on the aisle, halfway up the room. Seats were filling fast, and the panel participants were taking their places at the front of the room. Danielle parked her shoulder bag under the table and took the seat next to Astrid. She draped her purse over the back of the chair, while Randal sat down next to her. Odette and Nadine arrived, and they squished one more chair into the table, pushing Randal's shoulder against Danielle's.

"Just like old times," he joked in her ear, harkening back to their days in law school.

Astrid leaned forward, looking across Danielle to answer Randal. "At least we don't have to write the bar exam this time."

Randal gave her an easy smile.

The moderator spoke into the microphone, asking people to get settled, and the rest of the audience quickly took their seats.

Though the speakers were well-versed in their specialties, and the debate was lively, Danielle couldn't get her mind off Travis, wondering if he was still in the lobby, and what had brought him there in the first place.

Two hours in, when one of the audience members wandered off on an arcane point of law to do with protocols for the functioning of supranational tribunals, she gave in and slipped from her seat. Randal looked surprised and none too pleased at having to move his seat to let her pass. She took her purse but left her shoulder bag, letting everyone think she was going to the ladies' room.

She'd be right back. The odds that Travis was still out there were overwhelmingly small.

But, there he was.

One of the uniformed women had stepped out from behind the now-empty conference check-in desk and was talking and laughing with him. His gaze lifted, and he caught sight of Danielle. She stopped, not exactly sure what to do. She could still pretend she was going to the ladies' room, avoid even acknowledging him.

He didn't move, and neither did she.

Finally, she decided this was ridiculous. She wanted to know what he was doing here, and she'd go and ask him. She started across the mostly empty space, occupied only by hotel and conference staff, and the odd delegate who, like her, had stepped temporarily out of their session.

Her heels clicked on the marble floor. She was conscious of every step. Travis's face was impassive, but he kept watching as she grew closer.

"Sounds good," he said to the young, blonde woman. "I'll talk to you later."

Then he nodded to Danielle. "Hi there."

The woman watched over her shoulder with obvious curiosity as she moved back to the long registration table.

"What are you doing here?" Danielle asked without preamble.

"I was getting a coffee, but then Melanie and I started chatting."

Danielle cast a reflexive glance to the woman who wasn't even hiding her interest. "I meant, what are you doing at this hotel? You said you were at the Blonde Desert."

"When the Emperor Plaza found out I was a bull riding champion, they comped a suite."

"Did you flash your belt buckle?"

He grinned. "Never thought of that."

"How did they know?"

Travis nodded toward the closed door of the meeting room. "He in there with you?"

"You mean Randal?"

"You still think it's just business?"

"Absolutely." More than ever. In fact, she was

embarrassed now that she'd ever thought it might be something else.

Travis cracked a mocking half smile.

"What?"

"For such a smart woman, you're really not a very smart woman."

"Yeah? Well, for such a dumb cowboy, you really are a dumb cowboy."

If she'd hoped to get a rise out of him, it didn't work. His expression never faltered.

"You're reading way too much into this," she told him, glancing guiltily toward the meeting room, thinking she needed to get back there and catch the end of the session.

"No, I'm not," said Travis.

She decided to put a stop to the debate. "He's got a girlfriend back in D.C."

"Not a very good one."

Danielle folded her arms across her chest. "Now, that's just absurd. You don't know a single thing about her." Danielle didn't even know her name.

"I know he's thinking about cheating on her."

"You're clairvoyant as well as a bull rider?"

"You don't need to be clairvoyant to read lust in somebody's expression."

Danielle's thoughts faltered, taking her down a worrisome pathway. "Was it me?"

"That he's lusting after?"

"No. I mean, did I say something, or do something to make it look like I was interested in him?"

Travis rocked back ever so slightly. "*Are* you interested in him?"

"No. I mean, I don't think so. But I could be one of those women."

"One of what women?"

"The ones who don't want a guy, but don't want any other woman to have him, either. I mean, maybe when I heard he had a girlfriend, I subconsciously started getting jealous."

"You're not one of those women."

"How do you know for sure? I might be." What an incredibly distasteful character trait.

"It's not you. It's him. He sends out possessive vibes for about a hundred yards."

"We haven't seen each other in four years."

"Doesn't matter," Travis confidently drawled.

The sound of applause drifted through the walls. Seconds later, four sets of double doors opened across the lobby, people spilling out in a steady stream. She guessed that answered whether or not she was going to catch the end of the session.

"Here he comes," said Travis.

Danielle followed the trajectory of his gaze.

"Straight for you."

"He's got my bag."

"A convenient excuse."

"A gentlemanly act."

Travis coughed out a laugh.

"You just can't believe you might have it wrong," she challenged.

"He'll ask you to lunch," Travis predicted. "And when you tell him you're having lunch with me, it'll kill him. He'll say or do something to put me in my place. He'll be absolutely compelled to point out the cultural differences between you and me, and how he's the better man."

"I'm not going for lunch with you."

"Mark my words," said Travis as Randal arrived.

"You left your bag behind," said Randal, sparing a fleeting glance in Travis's direction.

"Thank you," Danielle offered, feeling a smug sense of satisfaction.

"Travis Jacobs," Travis introduced himself, holding out his hand.

Randal seemed to hesitate for a split second. "Randal Kleinfeld." He shook hands. "I went to Harvard with Danielle."

"So, I hear," said Travis.

Randal turned his attention back to Danielle. "So, what would you like to do for lunch?"

She could all but hear Travis's mocking thoughts,

feel him daring her to test his theory. If she did, she'd be stuck going to lunch with him. If she didn't, he'd probably never let her live it down. But when Randal didn't try to put Travis in his place the way Travis had predicted, Danielle would feel as if she'd won something, too.

It was worth a lunch with Travis, she decided.

"I'm so sorry," she told Randal. "But Travis and I have just made lunch plans."

Randal's attention darted briefly to Travis. His eyes narrowed as if he was none too happy. But when he spoke to Danielle, his expression smoothed out again.

"I thought you might like to hear about the rest of the tariff Q and A." Randal smiled, and his gaze slid to Travis again. "We could contrast tripartite arrangements pertaining to intra-regional trade distortions versus the harmonization of partner states."

"We're going to contrast the black bulls with the white ones," Travis said with a straight face.

Danielle thought it was a stretch for Travis to take Randal's words as a slight, but she nearly laughed at the comeback.

"I can make some introductions to people at the firm," Randal pushed on. "You should use the break time to your advantage."

"Sorry," said Danielle. "But I already have plans."

Randal hit Travis with a disparaging look. "You're going to take advantage of her good manners?"

"I was going to pay for the lunch," said Travis.

"That's not the point."

Danielle reached out to where Randal held her bag. "Thanks for bringing this. I'll probably see you later on in the day?"

Before Randal could react, Travis removed the bag from his grasp.

"Jacque Alanis Signature Room?" Travis asked her in a clear voice, naming the most exclusive and expensive restaurant on the Strip. Then he took her arm and deftly turned her for the main entrance.

"You're the one who's throwing down the gauntlet," she accused as they moved out of earshot.

"If his motives are pure, he'll have no interest in which restaurant we choose."

"We're going to contrast the black and white *bulls?*"

"He tossed out all that technical language for my benefit."

"Lawyers always talk that way."

"You don't."

Danielle tried to decide if he was right. "I do when I'm with other lawyers."

"You don't do it to belittle other people in a conversation."

She thought about that. "Sometimes I do it to you."

He seemed to ponder the comment as they walked out the doors of the main entrance. "Sometimes I deserve it."

Danielle gaped at him in astonishment, as he gave a hand signal to a doorman.

Within moments, a long, white limousine was pulling to the curb, and the porter held open the back door.

"You have got to be kidding," she told Travis.

"He's still watching. I want to make this good."

Danielle didn't believe that for one minute. "By now, Randal's gone to lunch with someone else."

"No, he hasn't." Travis guided her forward with a hand on the small of her back. "And the more I look like a rival, the faster he'll tip his hand, and prove me right. He's still after you."

She put her hand on the open car door. "This is going to cost you a fortune."

"You're talking to a man with bull riding prize money in his jeans."

"You're going to spend it all just to make a point?"

"Might as well spend it on you." His blue eyes were fixed and determined.

She gave an unconcerned shrug, answering as she

slid into the car. "Fine. I've got nothing against the Jacque Alanis Signature Room."

Travis grinned and slipped the doorman a bill before following her inside. The door shut behind him, and his phone began to ring. He reached into the breast pocket of his Western shirt.

"I think the Signature Room requires a jacket," said Danielle.

He gazed at his phone display. "In the absence of a jacket, they require a good tip." He gave her an eyebrow waggle. "It's Vegas, baby. You mind if I take this? It's Caleb."

Danielle felt her eyes widen. She wondered how Caleb could have known she was with Travis. Then she remembered Caleb and Travis were close friends. Then she realized she was making a colossal mistake by accepting his invitation to lunch. This was Travis, her archenemy from Lyndon Valley. Why had she let her guard down?

"Hey, Caleb," he said into the phone.

Then he paused and listened, brow furrowing in concern.

The driver put the limo into gear and pulled ahead.

"Is everybody okay with that?" he asked.

Danielle didn't want to be nosey, but she couldn't

help think something was wrong back at the Jacobses' ranch.

"No. If that's what he wants, then it seems like a good solution." Travis paused again. "Yeah. Sure. I'll get it done."

The limo pulled into the busy street, and Danielle hung on to a handle as they bumped from the hotel driveway. The Signature Room was only half a mile away, but traffic was busy.

Travis's gaze went to Danielle, a conspiratorial smile growing on his face. "She's here? Really?"

She held her breath, not exactly sure why she wanted Caleb kept in the dark, but quite certain that she did.

"I'll watch for her," said Travis. "Thursday, it is. See you then."

He ended the call. Then he grinned at her. "Caleb just informed me you were in Vegas."

Danielle struggled to frame the right words. She didn't want to offend Travis, but she didn't want anybody getting the wrong idea, either.

"Relax," he drawled. "I'm not going to kiss and tell."

Her guilt turned to irritation. "Nobody's kissing anyone."

"It's an expression."

Her own phone chimed.

He glanced to her purse. "Go for it. I did."

"Thanks." She popped the snap and reached inside, extracting the slim phone. It was Caleb.

She pressed the answer button, watching Travis as she spoke. "Hi, Caleb."

Travis's brows shot up. Then he grinned, shaking his head.

"How's the conference?" Caleb asked.

"Interesting, so far," said Danielle, thinking it was interesting, and on more than one level. "It's going very well," she added.

"Good. Glad to hear it. Listen, I'm going to be in Vegas on Thursday."

Danielle shot a reflexive and accusatory glare at Travis. He could have mentioned that fact.

"You're coming to Vegas," she said to both men.

"We're going to hold Alex Cable's bachelor party there. You remember he's marrying Mandy's cousin Lisa?"

"I do," Danielle confirmed.

Caleb's wife, Mandy, had only recently discovered Lisa was her cousin. Lisa was Mayor Seth Jacobs's Chief of Staff, and Danielle had worked with her on permitting for the Lyndon Valley railway. Alex also had a family connection. He was Mandy's brother-in-law Zach's partner in DFB Brewing Company.

"We were going to hold it at the brewery, but they ran into a problem with some renovations, so we're moving to plan B. Hey, you'll never guess who else is in Vegas this weekend."

"Who?" she asked, her voice going slightly high pitched as guilt contracted her stomach.

"Travis. He's going to plan everything, and we'll fly in Thursday afternoon. I'd like to meet with you about the Columbia accounting firm and a couple of other things if you can still be there."

"Sure," said Danielle. "No problem." She had planned to fly back to Chicago on Tuesday, but Action Equipment was a very important client. She'd meet Caleb whenever and wherever he needed.

"He's bull riding," said Caleb.

"Travis?"

"Mandy saw where he won yesterday."

"Good for him," said Danielle.

"You're at the Emperor Plaza?"

"I am," she admitted.

"I'll see if Travis can get our rooms there."

"Good idea."

"Perfect. Talk to you Thursday."

"Bye, Caleb." She pushed the end button, letting her hand drop into her lap.

Travis's phone rang.

"That'll be Caleb," she told him fatalistically. "He wants you to get them rooms at the Emperor Plaza."

Travis grinned. "Hi, Caleb."

The limo took a wide turn, and Danielle hung on again. It then came to a smooth stop in front of the restaurant entrance.

"Sure," said Travis. "I'll send the particulars as soon as I have them. You want strippers?"

Danielle shot him a glower of disapproval.

Travis chuckled into the phone. "Yeah, that's what I thought. I wouldn't want to tangle with her either."

The driver pulled opened the limo door, letting sunshine and warm air flood in. The noise from other traffic and the sidewalk crowds displaced the relative quiet of the limo.

"Gotta go," said Travis. "I've got a hot lunch date."

"Very funny," Danielle muttered as she shifted to the door.

"Ma'am," said the driver, holding out his hand.

She accepted the offer of assistance, smoothing her skirt as she stepped onto the sidewalk. Travis climbed out, her bag in his hand.

He paid the driver. Then he generously tipped the maître d', and they were quickly shown to a table on the second-floor patio. They had a sun umbrella above them, flower boxes decorating the rail beside them, and a panoramic fountain display across the street. The white tablecloth billowed slightly in the breeze, held down by a low, floral centerpiece and an abundant setting of fine china, crystal and silver.

It was warm, and Danielle shrugged out of her gray blazer. The waiter offered to hang it up, and laid a linen napkin across her lap.

She glanced at her watch to see it was coming up on noon. "I need to get back by one-thirty."

"No problem," said Travis, accepting a slim, leather-bound menu from the waiter.

The man handed Danielle a menu, while a second waiter filled their glasses with distilled water. The traffic noise and stereo music wafted up to them, along with laughter and a few yelps from the crowds below as the fountains danced higher. It was only noon, but many youthful tourists were already in the party spirit.

"Tell me you were joking about the strippers," said Danielle, focusing her attention across the table.

"I was joking about the strippers."

"That didn't sound sincere."

"If Alex wanted strippers, I'd get him strippers."

"Would you want them at your bachelor party?"

"Nope." There wasn't the slightest hesitation in his answer.

"Are you humoring me?"

"No."

"Are you sure?"

The Travis she'd observed over the past two years was ribald and rowdy. She could easily picture him whooping it up at a bachelor party.

He sat forward, resting his forearms on the table and fixing his gaze on her. "If I was getting married, I expect I'd be seeing a gorgeous woman naked on a regular basis. I wouldn't have the slightest interest in anyone else."

Danielle had to give him points for that. "Good answer."

"Thank you. I'm not without experience."

"Seeing naked women?" she joked.

"Falling in love."

That answer threw her. "You're in love?"

Travis was in a relationship? What had she missed? And why had a knot suddenly formed in her stomach?

"I watched Caleb, Reed, Seth and Alex all fall head over heels in love. I think I know what to expect."

"But you're not in love yourself?"

"Not yet." His expression turned reflective. "But if it happens, I know I'll recognize the signs."

The knot in her stomach relaxed.

"Your turn," he told her, his inquiring tone putting her on alert. "Ever been in love?"

Unsure how much she wanted to disclose to Travis, she bought herself a moment, reaching for two of the flowers in the centerpiece, switching their places to fix the balance.

"I've dated men I liked," she allowed. "Some, I liked very much. But love?" She shook her head. "I probably wouldn't know the signs if they bit me on the backside."

"I can tell you the signs," Travis offered easily. "Or I can bite you on the backside. Your choice."

A rush of unexpected arousal raised the temperature on her skin.

Travis grinned. "You're blushing."

"I'm embarrassed. You're far too crude."

"No." He waggled his brows. "I'm exactly the right amount of crude."

Danielle couldn't help remembering Nadine's brazen comments. Crude could be sexy. Crude could be very, very sexy.

# Three

When Travis spotted Danielle across the lobby that evening, he knew his hunch had paid off. Randal was with her, as he'd expected. They were part of a larger group that included her friends Astra, Nadine and Odette, obviously gathering together before leaving for a function.

She was dressed in a black cocktail dress. He wouldn't call it basic. It was off the shoulder, with a lace trimmed neckline that sparkled with inset jewels. The hammered satin molded to her breasts, fitting her waist, and flowed smoothly down to midthigh. She wore delicate diamond earrings, and a thin, diamond choker.

Her shoes were silver, barely there, with long, thin

heels that made him want to peel them off and toss them in the corner of his hotel room.

Randal clearly felt the same way. The man was practically salivating as he gazed at her shapely legs. Danielle was slender, very much suited to elegant clothes. But, with big, brown eyes and full, red lips, she looked sophisticated one minute, innocent the next. A man didn't know whether to protect her or ravish her. Travis wanted to do both.

While the group chatted, he made his way closer. He'd picked up a suit in one of the hotel shops. It was basic, charcoal-gray, with a white shirt and silver striped tie. His hair was trimmed neat, his face clean-shaven. The only thing that differentiated him from the lawyers in the room was a pair of polished, black cowboy boots.

"Travis," Nadine sang out, motioning him over. "Look, Danielle. It's Travis."

Danielle spotted him, and her round eyes went wider still. It might have been the shock of having him show up unexpectedly, but he hoped it was surprise at how well he'd cleaned up.

He'd made her at least an hour late for her workshops this afternoon. He should have felt guilty about that, but he didn't. They hadn't made any plans to see each other again. But he'd guessed that whatever evening shindig was being put on by the conference would start in the lobby.

Nadine skipped over and gave him a friendly hug. She was dressed in deep purple with lots of sequins.

She pulled back. "You look terrific."

"Thanks." He made a show of taking in her dress and her dangling earrings. "You look very beautiful yourself."

She gave a delighted grin at the compliment.

His gaze moved to Danielle, catching Randal's scowl on the way by, and experiencing a thrill of satisfaction.

"Good evening, Danielle."

"Travis," she acknowledged evenly, an unspoken question in her eyes. She likely wanted to know what on earth he was doing.

"Nice to see you again, Randal." He nodded to the man. "Astra, Odette." His gaze paused on a thin, expensively dressed, older woman, standing next to a man who looked to be her husband.

"Claude and Catherine Hedley," Danielle introduced. "This is Travis Jacobs. Travis is from Lyndon Valley, Colorado. He's a friend of Caleb Terrell, Active Equipment, one of my major clients."

Catherine Hedley gave a warm smile. "So nice to meet you, Mr. Jacobs. Are you attending the conference?"

Travis stepped forward to gently shake the older woman's hand. "Please, call me Travis. I'm not a lawyer, ma'am."

Randal piped up. "He's a bull rider."

Claude Hedley looked surprised by the revelation.

"I'm a rancher, sir." Travis held out his hand to Claude. "Our spread is next door to Caleb's in Lyndon Valley."

"And he won first prize last night," Odette put in helpfully.

"Caleb diversified into Active Equipment many years ago," Danielle elaborated, obviously trying to make up for the social gaffe of being acquainted with a bull rider. "While the Jacobs family has gone into politics, the arts in New York, and a fast-growing international brewing company."

"The brewery is my brother-in-law," said Travis, unwilling to push the spin too far. "I just take care of the cattle."

Claude Hedley shook his hand. "Call me Claude. It sounds like your family is up and coming."

"His sister is Katrina Jacobs," said Astra. "The ballet dancer."

Travis glanced at her in surprise.

"I've got internet," said Astra.

"Danielle, your friend should join us for the reception," Catherine Hedley put in. Then she looked to Travis. "We're touring the Van Ostram Botanical Gardens."

Randal obviously couldn't hold his tongue. "I'm sure Travis has plans with the rodeo crowd."

"As a matter of fact," said Travis, glancing at his watch. "I just had a meeting postponed."

"That settles it," said Catherine with another smile. "You know, I do believe I've seen your sister dance."

"She's been with the Liberty Ballet for several years now."

"That makes sense, then."

"We can catch the limos out front," Claude offered, stretching out an arm to invite them to proceed.

Randal swiftly sidled up to Danielle. They were slightly ahead of Travis as the group began to move.

"What are you doing?" Randal hissed at her in clear annoyance.

"What do you expect me to do?"

"Get rid of him."

"How would you suggest I do that?"

Travis couldn't tell whether Danielle thought getting rid of him was a good idea or not. It didn't really matter, since he wasn't going anywhere except with her. Randal might be able to snow Danielle about his intentions, but Travis was on to him, and he was going to force the man to show his hand.

"You need their support," said Randal.

"They've already made me an offer," Danielle countered.

"Getting through the door is only the first step."

"Catherine invited him, not me."

"Everything the man says and does tonight will reflect on you."

Travis bit his tongue. He was tempted to tell Randal he'd do his level best not to spit and swear in front of the Hedleys. But he didn't want Randal to know he could overhear.

The group was forced to split up, taking two of the black Escalade SUVs. Randal jockeyed hard, but ended up with the Hedleys and Odette, where he politely, if reluctantly, offered to clamber into the third-row seat.

Travis intended to do the same in the other vehicle, but Nadine insisted that she, Astrid and Danielle could fit in the middle seat, and Travis should ride up front. The driver slanted a covetous glance at the three beautiful women in his rearview mirror and gave Travis a discrete thumbs-up as they pulled away.

When Astrid expressed a desire for breath mints, Travis asked the driver to stop and hopped out to buy them for her. He took enough time to be certain the Hedleys' group would have headed into the reception by the time the second Escalade arrived at the gardens.

Travis tipped the driver and helped each of the women out of the vehicle. The trees at the entrance were lit with tiny white lights. Glowing orange lanterns illuminated a stone walkway, while colored spots gave a fantasy aura to the leafy plants and flowering gardens.

Danielle moved up beside him as they passed a glowing, purple pond. "What exactly are you doing?"

Travis considered a range of answers and decided to be honest. "I'm making him stark raving mad."

"Why? I'm sure you had far better things to do tonight than hang out with a bunch of stuffy lawyers."

"You're not a stuffy lawyer."

"You know what I mean."

"He's going to show his hand, Danielle. He can't stand the competition, and he's going to make a pass at you. And then you'll know."

"Know what?"

Travis counted off on his fingers. "That he's willing to cheat on his girlfriend. That this was never about a job. That he wants you back in his life, back in his bed."

She went silent for a long moment. "It's not true."

"Yes, it is."

"Why do you even care?"

The question stopped Travis. It took him a minute to collect his thoughts. "I care because he's lying to you."

They walked a bit farther in silence, beneath a canopy of oaks, green, red and blue spots glowing up their trunks.

Finally, she drew an audible breath. "What you're doing doesn't make sense, Travis."

"Why does it have to make sense?" Even as he said the words, he knew she was right. He had absolutely no reason to meddle in her life.

"Everything has to make some kind of sense," she countered.

"Maybe to a lawyer. But cowboys operate on instinct."

She paused at the bottom of the stairs that led up to the pavilion, turning to face him. Astrid and Nadine were several yards ahead.

"And, what's your instinct telling you?" she asked.

He gazed down at her. His instinct was telling him to kiss her, and kiss her hard. But he couldn't do that here. Not that he could do it anywhere.

"It's telling me he's no good for you, Danielle. He's no good for you, and I'm the only guy around to stop him."

"I am a grown woman, Travis. I can stop him all by myself."

Travis smiled at that. In many ways it was true. But his way was faster, and he didn't like the odds that she'd end up getting hurt. "He's too sneaky, and you're too kind."

"What do you mean I'm kind? I fight with you *all* the time."

"It's safe for you to fight with me."

She tilted her pretty head sideways, and he couldn't help but think it was the perfect angle to kiss. "Your instincts telling you that, too?" she asked tartly.

"Yep. And they're infallible." He offered her his arm to walk up the staircase.

Inside the reception, Danielle left Travis to his own devises. She quickly found herself swept up in a whirlwind of introductions and conversations with the who's who of Nester and Hedley. It seemed they were interested in her South American experience. Brazil and Columbia were rising on everyone's trade radar in D.C., and their expertise was weak for the region. They saw an opportunity to get in early on this new wave, and they wanted Danielle to head up an entire division.

It was a genuine, exciting offer that didn't appear to have anything to do with Randal. In fact, she'd barely seen him since they arrived. The senior partners seemed to know her entire professional history, even details of Caleb's Active Equipment activities and challenges in Columbia.

It was close to eleven when, throat raw from talking over the music, and feet sore from her high shoes, she pushed her way up to a bar stool and asked the bartender for a soda and lime.

"He's watching you," came Travis's deep voice from behind her left ear. He took the stool next to her.

"He's barely said a word to me all night long. Honestly, the only person creeping me out here, is you."

"He's known where you were every second."

She angled toward him. "First, I don't believe you. Second, I've been talking with his bosses. They're the ones who have his attention, not me."

Travis reached for a handful of the snack mix on the bar. "Keep telling yourself that."

"I will, thank you very much."

The waiter set her drink down in front of her and looked to Travis for his order.

"Are you hungry?" Travis asked her. "Those little crab puffs and cheese squares didn't do it for me."

"I'm not leaving yet."

"I'll take a beer," Travis said to the waiter. "Whatever you've got on tap."

"It's by the bottle, sir."

Danielle couldn't help but grin as she stirred the ice in her soda and lime.

"Anything from DFB?"

"Mountain Red?"

"Sounds great."

The waiter turned to the glass-fronted refrigerator.

"This isn't a honky-tonk," Danielle pointed out.

"Are my country roots showing?"

She realized how snobby she sounded. "An honest mistake. No big deal."

The waiter returned with an open bottle of Mountain Red and a chilled pilsner glass. Travis handed him a tip, and Danielle realized she was the one who lacked class.

"How's it going?" Travis asked her as he tipped the glass and poured in the amber liquid. It foamed slightly at the top of the flared glass.

"They seem serious," she answered, gazing at the bubbles in her own drink. "They know a lot about me."

"Yeah? All good?"

She smiled to herself. "They think it's good. They know what I did for Active Equipment and a few others, and they want me to head up a South American division."

She couldn't help replaying the conversations in her mind. If Claude Hedley was to be believed, she'd be on the cutting edge of a global wave of interest. The earning potential would be massive, and she'd be in a position to set her own priorities and parameters.

"You going to take it?" asked Travis.

"I'm thinking about it," she answered honestly. Then it suddenly occurred to her she was talking to a close friend of Caleb's.

She quickly turned to take in his expression. "But…uh…"

He caught on quick. "You don't want me to tell Caleb."

Her hand went reflexively to his forearm. "I'd never ask you to lie. But it would be better for me if you didn't mention it to him right away."

He took a reflective drink of his beer. "Your secret's safe with me."

"Thank you. I'm sorry to put you in that position."

"I know you didn't do it on purpose."

"I really didn't think this through." Where had

her common sense been yesterday when she'd mentioned this to Travis.

"Unusual for you?" he asked.

"Very."

"He's coming over."

"Who?"

"Randal. Who else." Travis's gaze went down. "You're touching me, and he feels threatened. He's about to stake his territory."

She immediately realized she hadn't taken her hand from Travis's arm. Then she realized his arm was warm, hot actually under her fingertips. He was solid, strong and alive. She didn't want to pull away.

"Don't panic," Travis muttered in an undertone. "But I'm going to touch your hair."

"Wha—"

Before she could finish the word, he gently brushed the back of his knuckles along her cheek, smoothing her hair back over her ear.

She froze, every nerve ending in her body focusing on the gentle touch. Pings of awareness and desire shot out, sending signals of desire to every corner of her body.

"Dani," boomed Randal's voice. He wrapped a hearty arm around her shoulders and gave her a pat. "It looked like things went well?"

Travis's hand fell away. "Hello, Randal."

"Oh, Travis." Randal pretended he'd just noticed him. "How're you holding up here?"

"Managing just fine," Travis responded.

Randal turned his attention back to Danielle. "What did they say? More importantly, what did *you* say?"

"She hasn't made up her mind yet," Travis put in.

Randal sent him a glare. "I asked Dani."

"Well, *Dani* told me first."

"Travis," Danielle warned.

He was entitled to whatever theory he concocted, but that didn't give him the right to pick a fight.

Randal drew back his shoulders, lifting his chin. "She did, did she?"

"They offered me a South American division," she quickly told Randal.

"That's great." His shoulders relaxed. "I'm going to head up Europe, starting in September. We'd be at exactly the same level, on the partners' floor. I don't have to tell you, that's an impressive way to enter the firm."

"You don't have to tell me," Danielle agreed.

"The expense account is unlimited. The benefits are top-drawer, and the work is some of the most intellectually stimulating—"

"Randal?" she interrupted.

"Yes?"

"I've been listening to the sales pitch all night." Travis stifled a chuckle.

Randal's attention immediately flew to him. "You got something to add here?"

"Not a thing," said Travis, polishing off his beer. "You're doing just fine all by yourself."

Randal glared a moment longer, but then something caught his attention across the room. "There's old man Nester." He squeezed Danielle's shoulder, lowering his voice to a conspiratorial level. "Give me three minutes to break into the conversation, then come over and join us."

He walked away.

Travis looked at Danielle, and she stared back.

"Well?" he asked.

She was all schmoozed out. Her feet were swelling. Her makeup was about to crack. And the last thing she wanted to do was humor the wheezy, narcissistic Edger Nester through what she'd heard tended to be half-hour-long discourses on the flaws in judicial procedure. If she took the job, she'd have to put up with it. But she wasn't there yet.

"I'm out of here," she told Travis.

His hand went immediately to her elbow, helping her down from the high stool, before turning them to a nearby side exit.

They came out into the gardens, quiet in the late hour. The breeze had picked up, cooling the air, and Travis quickly shrugged out of his suit jacket, draping it around her shoulders. They started down a winding flagstone walkway.

"That was a quick decision," he noted.

"I've only met Mr. Nester once, but I've heard tales of his boring orations, and I'm tired." She reached down and peeled off her sandals, moving to the soft grass at the side of the path. "My feet are killing me."

"You want me to carry you?" he offered.

She shook her head, though the thought of being held in his arms gave her a shiver of excitement. "This is nice." She curled her toes into the dense blades of grass.

He took up a slow pace, along the edge of a narrow brook, in the general direction of a purple lighted pond, leaving the music and laughter behind them. "If you resign, what will happen in Chicago?"

"You mean, what will happen to Active Equipment?"

"And your other clients."

"They'll be assigned to other lawyers."

"Does that worry you?"

"I'd feel guilty," she admitted, switching her sandals to the other hand. "But I'm not the only law-yer in the world. My firm has many other people who are perfectly capable of servicing my clients."

"So, there's nothing unique about you?"

She smiled at that. "I'd like to think there was. I'd like to think I was irreplaceable. But that would be a little conceited, right?"

His voice was low, sounding almost annoyed. "Some people *do* have to stay where they're needed."

"Do you think I'm letting Caleb down?"

"I wasn't talking about you."

She paused, tilting her head to peer up at him. "Who?"

He stopped walking, seeming to hesitate for a long moment, as the babble of the brook rose around them, the scent of the flowers sweetened the air. "I was talking about me."

"You're leaving Lyndon Valley?" She could hardly believe it.

In her mind, Travis *was* Lyndon Valley. While the Terrells and the other Jacobs siblings might come and go from the ranches, Travis was the stalwart, always there, always available, always taking care of anything and everything.

He shook his head. "My point was, I *can't* leave Lyndon Valley. The ranch needs me."

"And you need the ranch." She thought she understood.

"Something like that." There was an edge to his voice.

"You think I'm abandoning the people who count on me."

It was hardly the same situation. Just because she'd gone to law school and started in a particular job, didn't mean she had to stay there forever.

"If you were abandoning them. If they told you, you were abandoning them. If you knew it would hurt them, would you stay?"

"That's a hypothetical situation." She'd like to think she'd done some good work for Caleb and the others over the years. But she'd hardly cripple anyone's business if she moved on.

"Hypothetically speaking, and I'm not going to hold you to it, if you knew it would hurt them, would you leave anyway?"

She searched his expression. "What are you getting at, Travis?"

He gazed at the lighted trees. "Responsibility, I guess—the kind of responsibility that paints a man into a corner and limits his choices."

She stepped forward, still not pinning down where he was going with this. "You're getting very philosophical on me, cowboy."

He gave a self-conscious smile. "Just trying to help you make a decision."

"You want me to stay in Chicago."

"I want you to understand the true details of your options."

A door banged shut on the pavilion, and several voices rose in the garden.

"He wouldn't come looking for me," Danielle said, more to herself than to Travis.

"Oh, yes, he would." Travis snagged her hand, striding across the sloped grass, tugging her toward a dark corner where they'd be screened from the path.

She had to trot to keep up.

They made their way behind a hedge, beyond the orange glow of the walkway lanterns, to a secluded corner where blue light filtered weakly through the maple leaves. Her mind went back over his words. He'd said it limited a man's choices, not a woman's choices, not a person's choices.

He abruptly stopped, and she nearly ran into him.

"Your feet okay?" he asked, turning.

"Travis, do you *want* to leave the ranch?"

"No."

She pondered a second longer. "But you resent that you can't. Or, wait a minute, you resent that you don't have the choice."

This time he hesitated before answering.

"You should tell them," she said.

"Tell them what?"

"That you—"

"That Katrina can't be a ballerina?" Travis spoke right over her, annoyance in his tone. "That Seth should give up being mayor? That Mandy can't be in Chicago with Caleb? Or that Abigail should force Zach to sell his brewery?"

Danielle definitely saw his point. It didn't make it fair, but she understood how he must feel.

"We're the fifth generation," he told her.

"That's a lot on your shoulders."

"They're broad shoulders."

Her gaze strayed. "Yes, they are."

"You won't say anything to Caleb."

"And mess with your self-righteous sense of nobility?"

"I'm not self-righteous."

She gazed up into his eyes. He was taller when her feet were bare. Taller, stronger, magnificent.

"You are noble," she whispered, finding herself shifting closer to him.

"I'm practical."

"You operate on instinct," she reminded him, tilting her chin, moistening her lips, wondering if she could possibly be more obvious.

"I do," he breathed.

"So, instinctively…"

His hands bracketed her hips, easing her against him. "Instinctively, I want to kiss you."

She smiled.

"But I've had that particular instinct for a long time now, and I'm not sure I should trust it."

"You should trust it."

His hands moved to her face, cradling it gently in his palms. "What about my other instincts?"

"You have other instincts?"

"To toss you down on the grass and ravish you in the moonlight."

Want and need instantly cascaded through her, weakening her knees and robbing her of her breath. She wished it didn't sound so tempting. There were a million complicated reasons to keep her distance from Travis, even if her own desires were screaming at her to ignore them.

She came up on her toes to meet him. "Let's take it one instinct at a time."

"Yes, ma'am." His lips came down on hers, warm and firm, fueled with purpose and expectation.

One arm went around her waist, the other bracing the back of her head. She dropped her sandals and clung to his shoulders. Then she ran her hands through his hair, pressing her body against his, parting her lips and inviting the sweep of his tongue.

His kiss deepened, and she clung tighter, letting the sweep of arousal and desire flood through her. Leaves clattered above them. A blue glow surrounded them. The grass was cool on her feet, while Travis's hot palm moved its way down her cheek, to her neck, to the bare shoulder revealed by her dress.

He stopped there, fingertips caressing against her skin.

He broke the kiss and pulled back, breathing deeply.

She had to blink the world back into focus.

"We have to stop now." His tone was slightly ragged.

"I know." She understood that they were playing with fire.

He stepped determinedly back, letting his hold drop away from her, putting space between them.

When he spoke again, his deep voice rumbled through her. "I guess that was inevitable."

"Kissing me?"

He held her gaze in the dim light. "Well, that, too. But I was thinking it was inevitable that kissing you would be fantastic."

*Fantastic?* She loved that word. Her skin glowed.

Her lips tingled. Every inch of her body felt the sensual impact of Travis.

Still, *fantastic* didn't quite do it justice.

# Four

"*That* was fantastic," Travis shouted to Corey as he clambered out of the dusty dune buggy in the parking lot of Desert High Rentals. He peeled off his crash helmet, calling again. "I think we've found a winner."

Corey gave him the thumbs-up as he stepped away from his own tube-style, open-air vehicle. It had once been red, but now was plastered with dirt and debris from their twenty-mile race across the desert.

"It's a toss-up between this and paintball," said Corey.

The two men started toward the compact, white-painted building and the chain-link compound that held neat rows of rental dune buggies.

"I was trying to figure out if we'd have time to do both," Travis added.

When Travis had called Corey this morning, Corey had quickly agreed to help out. So, they'd spent the day testing activities for the upcoming bachelor party.

Hot air ballooning had been a bust—too sedentary. Sky diving was another option, but they couldn't count on everyone buying into that. They'd looked into bus and boat tours, and even gambling, but Travis was pretty sure thrills and adrenaline was the way to go.

A keg of beer, spicy, fried junk food and the Colorado Rockies game on the big screen at the Emperor Plaza's Ace High Lounge was a given. Travis had booked it for the private party Friday night.

"How early will these guys be willing to get up?" Corey asked.

"They're mostly cowboys. But I guess it depends on how it goes Thursday night—whether things stay down to a dull roar. Caleb's pilot is flying everybody in around four."

Thursday would be informal. They'd stop by a bar or two along the Strip, maybe play a little poker.

"Book paintball for the morning," said Corey. "If they get blasted the night before, they can bloody well cowboy up."

Travis grinned. Better to have too much planned than too little.

"Paintball, it is," agreed Travis. "Followed by dune buggy racing in the afternoon, and then Ace High for the night."

"The guys can all crawl to their rooms from there."

"We should have been party planners," said Travis as he set his helmet down on the counter, in the shade of the porch at the rental building.

"Party planners don't get the girls," Corey responded.

"How'd it go out there?" asked the rotund, fifty-something clerk as he set his magazine down and stood to meet them.

"Great," Travis replied. "It's a very exciting course. We're looking to bring a group back with us on Friday afternoon."

The man pulled a clipboard down from a hook on the wall and rustled up a pen from a drawer beneath the counter. "How many in your group?"

"About thirty. Better make it thirty-five to be safe."

The man's bushy brows went up. "Thirty guys? Do they each need their own buggy?"

"I'd plan on that," said Travis.

The man stepped away, opening a back door to

shout outside. "Micky. Can you do thirty-five for Friday afternoon?"

The response was muffled.

"Well, call the parts store. Get them to overnight freight."

Another muffled response.

Travis glanced at Corey, who made a show of crossing his fingers. "We don't want to go with the river boat tour."

"Not unless they can guarantee models in bikinis."

"And that zip line seemed pretty lame."

Travis agreed. Though it sounded exciting to soar suspended hundreds of feet above the ground, in reality, it had been more like an amusement park ride. You had no control over anything that happened. You just hung there and watched the scenery go by.

The dune buggy man turned back to them. "We can cover you." He made a notation on his clipboard. "If this is a corporate event, you better check your insurance." He handed Travis a written brochure.

Travis glanced at it without reading. "If it's a private event?"

The man gave a gap-toothed grin. "Better buy

yourself some event insurance. This ain't covered under your regular homeowner's policy."

"Then I guess it's a corporate event," said Travis. "Can we bring a credit card with us Friday?"

"Sure thing." The man glanced at today's rental agreement. "Mr. Jacobs."

Travis reached out to shake the man's hand. "Thanks for your help."

With a nod, Corey slid his helmet across the counter, and they turned to step off the low porch.

"There's a place called South Rim, partway back on the highway," said Corey as they crossed the asphalt parking lot under the scorching sun. "It's pretty laid-back, burgers and steaks. About a dozen beers on tap. Might work for lunch on Friday. You want to check it out?"

"Sure," Travis agreed, pressing the unlock button on his rented SUV. "I could absolutely go for a beer."

It was nearly five o'clock, and his other option was going back to the hotel. If he went back to the hotel, he was sure he'd go against his better judgment and start hunting around for Danielle.

It had been a mistake to kiss her last night. He knew it then, and he knew it now. But a man could only take so much. And being alone in the dark with a beautiful, desirable woman, who scoffed at the right moments, laughed at the right moments and gazed up at him with huge, dark bedroom eyes, well, kissing her had been inevitable.

He levered into the driver's seat and started the engine, peeling out of the parking lot and onto the road.

He'd relived the kiss about a thousand times already. Then he'd thought about doing it again, thought about doing even more, then he'd pulled himself ruthlessly back. Danielle was Danielle, the same woman he'd fought with for months. She had a professional relationship with his brother-in-law Caleb, another one with his sister Katrina for the Sasha Terrell Fund.

Nothing had changed between them. He'd found Danielle sexy as soon as he'd met her. She found him coarse and unrefined. She didn't like his sense of humor, thought his perspective was limited, thought he was and always would be a hick cowboy from backwater Colorado.

It was all true, and no amount of sexual attraction was going to change any of that. Which meant nothing more could happen between them.

He smacked a hand down on the steering wheel in frustration.

"What?" Corey turned to look.

"Nothing."

"You don't want to go to the South Rim?"

"The South Rim is fine. I'm hungry, and I'm damn sure thirsty."

"Well, okay, then."

Brimming with pent-up energy, Travis ignored the double line on the highway, pulling out to pass a semi as they wound up a hill. A pickup suddenly crested the rise, and he slammed the brakes, dumping his speed and pulling back behind the tractor trailer. Both the semi and the pickup driver leaned on their horns.

Corey gripped the handrail on the ceiling of the SUV. "Well. That was exciting."

"They need more passing lanes," Travis grumbled.

"We should have let you take another lap on the dune buggy." Corey sat back. "Work whatever the heck it is out of your system."

Travis knew what he needed to work this out of his system, and no motor vehicle could help him. He found his mouth flexing in a wry smirk. What he needed, he couldn't have.

"What?" Corey asked again.

The double lines ended, replaced by a single, broken line, and he ducked out to check for oncoming traffic. This time he could definitely make it. He stepped on the accelerator.

"I think whiskey's my best bet," he called to Corey as the engine revved higher.

"That sounds like girl trouble to me," Corey called back, hand gripping the handle again.

"It is girl trouble," Travis admitted.

"Back home?"

"In Vegas." He pulled back into the right lane, backing off and letting his speed drop down again.

"You've only been here two days."

"I work fast."

"Parking lot's coming up on your right. Past the motel and the park. The green sign."

Travis slowed, flipping on his signal light, and pulling to the shoulder so he wouldn't slow the semi down as it built up speed on the downhill grade.

The South Rim was a long, low brown building, perched on the side of a canyon. The floorboards on the deck squeaked under their boots as they made their way to an oversized, red door. Travis opened it to reveal a dim room with a polished, red wood bar, heavy tables and comfortable looking leather chairs, all surrounding three well-kept pool tables.

On the far side, glass doors led out to a deck that overlooked the canyon. The deck was dotted with low, planked tables and Adirondack chairs, turned toward the view. Vintage rock music gave a muted backdrop from overhead speakers, while the smell of grilling burgers hung in the air.

"Go ahead and grab a table," called a thirty-something woman from behind the bar. She was wearing a white blouse over a pair of black slacks, with her hair pulled back in a neat ponytail.

A dozen of the thirty or so tables were occupied, and a few people sat out on the deck. Two men shot a game at one of the pool tables. It was obviously an adult crowd, and conversation seemed cheerful and relaxed.

"You want to shoot a game?" asked Corey as he ambled toward a table.

"Sure." Travis dropped his hat on a chair and rolled up the sleeves of his white-and-gray checked shirt.

Realizing how much sand and dust had clung to him from the dune buggy ride, he headed for the men's room to take off a layer. Looking at himself in the mirror, he couldn't help but be impressed that none of the staff had turned their noses up as he and Corey walked in.

By the time he got back to the table, the waitress had produced glasses of ice water and a couple of menus. Travis ordered a beer and selected a pool cue.

"Hi there," came a soft female voice as a blond woman sauntered over to him. At a nearby table, a brunette closely watched the exchange.

"I'm Sandy," she introduced.

"Travis," he returned. "Nice to meet you."

The men's room door banged shut behind Corey. Then a smile lit his face as he approached the pool table.

"Corey," he introduced himself to the woman, holding out his broad hand.

"Sandy," she repeated. Then she turned to look at the brunette. "My friend is Linda."

"You gals from around here?" asked Corey.

She grinned. "We 'gals' are from California. San Diego. You?"

"I'm a bullfighter on the pro bull riding circuit."

"You're one of those guys with a red cape and a tight, gold-tassel-covered jacket?"

Travis coughed out a laugh at the image.

"That's in Spain, not in Nevada. I'm the guy in blue jeans who saves the cowboy's ass when the rangy brahma bull bucks him off and threatens to gore him or trample him." He gestured to Travis. "Guys like him. I saved his life on Saturday night."

Sandy looked to Travis. "That true?"

"It's true," Travis affirmed as he racked up the balls.

Linda rose from the table and wandered over. "You're a bull rider?" she asked Travis.

"I'm a rancher. Eight ball?" he asked Corey.

The waitress returned with Travis's beer, and Corey ordered one for himself. "Eight ball it is," he said to Travis. "So, what do you women do in San Diego?"

"We're caterers, mostly weddings, but corporate parties, too."

"Isn't that a coincidence." Corey took the break, hitting the racked balls hard and sending them shooting across the table. None went into a pocket. "We're planning a party right now."

"What kind of a party?" she asked.

"Bachelor party," said Corey.

"So, you'll be down on the Strip?"

"Part of the time," said Corey.

Travis called solids and took his first shot, putting away the six ball.

Corey gave a groan at the nice shot. "We're also doing paintball and dune buggy racing."

Travis couldn't help but hope Corey didn't mention their plans for lunch here. The women seemed nice enough, but this party wasn't going to be about pickups.

"Is one of you the groom?" asked Linda.

Corey grinned as he shook his head. "We're the party planners."

"The groom is a friend," said Travis. This time he sank the four.

"Am I being hustled?" asked Corey with obvious good humor.

"Does the groom live in Vegas?" asked Sandy.

"Colorado," answered Corey.

Travis missed the three, and Corey chalked his cue.

Sandy moved away from Corey, bringing her closer to Travis.

"So, Mr. Bull Riding Rancher, are you—"

"Would you like to order lunch?" The waitress's question interrupted.

Relieved, Travis turned his attention to the woman. "I'll take a cheeseburger."

"Same here," called Corey as he lined up on the ten ball. He pulled back his cue and made a perfect shot.

"Who's hustling who?" Travis joked, moving from the pool table to their dining table to take a drink of his beer.

He hadn't wanted Sandy to finish her purring question. He wasn't in the mood to flirt. His mind kept slipping to Danielle, wondering where she was, if Randal was with her, if he'd made a move on her.

Corey sank two balls in rapid succession. Then he missed, leaving a promising-looking table for Travis.

Conversation between Corey and the two women swirled around him, with the occasional burst of laughter. Travis worked his way through the rest of the solids, earning cheers from the women as he made a particularly tricky bank shot to sink the seven.

He easily finished up the eight ball to take the game.

"I guess you're buying lunch," he said to Corey as the waitress arrived with their burgers.

"You're the one with the good payday," Corey countered. "And I did—"

"I know. I know," Travis cut in. "You saved my life."

Travis returned his pool cue to the rack.

"Nice meeting you," he said to Sandy and Linda as he headed to sit down.

Corey obviously picked up on Travis's thinking. He also said goodbye, rather than asking the women to join them.

They hesitated slightly, but then returned to their own table.

"What the hell?" asked Corey as he swung into his chair across from Travis.

"I just want to eat." Travis stuffed a fry into his mouth then took another swallow of beer.

Corey frowned as he lifted his high-stacked burger. "After I did such a great job of chatting them up for you."

"They weren't really my type."

"Beautiful, friendly and built isn't your type?"

It was Travis's turn to frown. "Charming," he mocked.

"I think you'd better tell me a little more about this Vegas woman trouble. It's obviously cramping your style. Which wouldn't bother me much, except that it's blowing back on me."

"There's nothing to tell."

"Uh-huh." Corey's tone was clearly skeptical.

"She's hot, but she's off-limits."

"She's married?"

"Not married. There's a professional relationship to maneuver around. Two of them, actually."

"Can you fix them?"

"Nope."

"Then my advice to you is move on."

"That's what I'm doing."

Well, he'd move on as soon as he opened Danielle's eyes about Randal's motives. Travis losing didn't mean Randal got to win.

\* \* \*

The conference's windup golf tournament had finished, with Randal taking fourth place. Danielle suspected he could have done better, but he'd once confided in her that winning outright was a bad strategy for a young lawyer. In his estimation, it was better to be strongly competitive, but to let the senior people prevail, at least for a while.

The final dinner was in full swing, a gourmet buffet set up in the gardens of the hotel, the aromas of sage and rosemary from the steamer trays mingling with vanilla and cinnamon at the dessert display. White linen covered tables were illuminated by floodlights and torches.

At one of the many bars set up around the perimeter of the lawn, Danielle accepted another "superior court" drink. It was a special recipe invented by the hotel's chief bartender for the conference. It was a surprisingly delicious concoction of fruit juices, crushed ice, tequila and liquors. It was the final night of the conference. She planned to take advantage of the pool deck in the morning while her colleagues all flew home, so a little indulgence in liquor tonight suited her just fine.

"Thank you, Caleb," she muttered under her breath, toasting him in absentia. If he hadn't requested a meeting on Thursday, she wouldn't be in line for an impromptu mini vacation tomorrow.

Randal separated himself from the crowd, coming up beside her. "You didn't golf?" he opened.

He'd changed into suit and tie since the tournament ended, and now looked urbane and confident with a three-olive martini in one hand.

"That's because my golfing is not going to impress anyone."

"Nobody cares how well you golf at these things."

"Also," she elaborated, "I don't particularly like golf."

She sipped the frozen drink through a straw, while her lightweight dress rustled against her thighs in the night breeze.

"It's a great way to build relationships. Everybody who is anybody is out on the links at something like this."

"I was happier chatting with Astra."

Randal polished off the martini, exchanging the empty glass for a fresh drink as a waiter passed, taking an immediate sip. "Astra won't get you a partnership. Besides, you can chat with Astra any old time."

"She lives in New York." It wasn't very often the two women got the chance to see each other in person.

Randal frowned. "That's not what these things are for."

"You do realize that you care more about schmoozing and corporate climbing than most people."

"I care more than you do," Randal acknowledged. "But I don't care more than most people. Honestly, Dani, sometimes you are so naive."

"Naive? Are you serious?" She'd been called a lot of things in her lifetime, but never naive.

He took another sip of his drink, prompting her to do the same. The superior courts tasted best when they were ice-cold.

"You seem content to stand by and let people blow past you."

"What people?" she challenged.

He made an expansive gesture with one arm. "These people. All people. Well, all lawyers." He moved forward, dramatically lowering his voice, and she realized he must have had a few martinis before he got here. "You have a brilliant mind, Dani." His gaze focused on the neckline of her black-and-blue dress. "You have the whole package." He looked her in the eyes again. "But you seem singularly intent on wasting it."

She was starting to get annoyed. "I'm not wasting anything." She'd spent five years developing her knowledge of international law.

"When you hesitate. When Nester and Hedley make you a sweetheart of an offer, and you hesitate, do you know how that looks?"

"Like I'm prudent and conscientious?"

"Like you're indecisive and ungrateful."

"*Ungrateful?* Excuse me?"

His voice rose a little. "They're the top law firm in D.C., probably the most prestigious in the country."

"It's still a big decision," Danielle found herself feeling defensive. This time, she took a calming sip of her drink. Taste had nothing to do with it.

"What's to decide?" he demanded.

She listed off on her fingers. "To leave my firm. To leave my city. To leave my friends."

"You'll make new friends."

"I have some very good friends."

"Male friends?"

She frowned. "Some. What difference does it make?"

Randal shrugged and polished off his drink. "That sounds like it might be a boyfriend."

She pressed her lips together, thinking it was probably time to end the conversation.

"Is that what it is, Dani? You won't come to D.C. because of some guy you're sleeping with?"

"That's none of your business," Travis's voice interrupted as he loomed up next to Randal.

Randal twisted around to face him, his jaw clamping down. "This is a private party."

"Hello, Travis." Danielle couldn't help but feel grateful for his arrival.

"Hello, Danielle."

Randal's gaze darted from one to the other, settling on Travis. "How did you get in here?"

Travis kept his gaze on Danielle. "I flashed my belt buckle."

She couldn't help but grin.

"Everything okay?" Travis asked her.

Randal angled his body toward Travis. "That's none of *your* business."

"I'm fine," Danielle quickly put in, at the same time willing Travis to stay put. She had no desire to return to her conversation with Randal.

"Are you hungry?" Travis asked, seeming to read her mind. "Can I get you a fresh drink?"

"We're having a private conversation here," Randal firmly stated.

Travis's gaze slowly moved to Randal. "Yeah?"

"Yeah."

"Well, maybe you want to do that in a less pub-
lic place."

Randal turned to Danielle. "Let's go."

She didn't know how to react. She didn't want to
be rude to Randal, but she certainly didn't want to
leave the party with him.

"Aren't there more people you need to see?" she
asked, glancing around. Surely Randal wouldn't
give up an opportunity to schmooze.

"There's something I need to ask you." There was
a determination in his eyes.

"Right now?"

"Right now." He reached for her hand, twining
his fingers around hers.

She automatically pulled back, and his hand came
with hers.

Travis stepped forward, tone hard, words delib-
erate. "Let her go."

Randal held his ground, glaring at Travis. Both
men were still and silent for what seemed like a
full minute.

Finally, Randal let go of her hand.

He turned to Danielle. "I'd like to speak with
you."

"Let's do it later." She wasn't afraid of Randal,
but his behavior bordered on the bizarre.

He stared at her for another long moment.

"Fine," he ground out. "Later."

With a withering look at Travis, he turned to stalk away.

"That was weird," she couldn't help commenting. "You okay?"

"Perfectly fine." She shook off her feelings. "You?"

Travis grinned. "I've been to plenty of parties that ended in fights."

She shook her head at the ridiculous notion. "You weren't going to fight."

"He wasn't going to fight. I would have."

"You're incorrigible."

"Just from a different part of the country than him."

"What are you doing here?"

Randal had been right on that count, this was a private party, only the conference delegates had been invited. She doubted very much that flashing a bull riding belt buckle would have got Travis past security.

"Hedley invited me. Probably thanks to your exaggeration of my family's artistic and political success."

"That's how you play the game." She glanced down and noticed her drink glass was empty.

Travis noticed, too, and took it from her, quickly flagging down a passing waiter and handing it off.

"Thanks," she told him.

"Would you like another?" he asked.

"I think I will. Thanks to Caleb, I don't have to go to work in the morning."

"I was hoping to find you here," said Travis as they moved toward a nearby bar. "I need your advice on something,"

"You mean you didn't come to the party to mingle with lawyers and judges?" Out of the corner of her eye, she caught sight of Randal.

He was talking to one of the conference presenters. He glanced up, and their gazes met. She quickly looked away.

"As appealing as that sounds..." said Travis.

Danielle smiled at his sarcasm.

"I'm going to have to sign a contract on Thursday. I'm sure it'll be a simple matter for you, but I need to make sure I understand the liability."

She tried to switch to her lawyer brain, and quickly realized she was a little tipsy. "What kind of a contract?"

"Dune buggy racing."

She rested her hand on the bar and turned to peer at him. "Excuse me?"

"For the bachelor party. Thirty or so guys are all

going dune buggy racing. Either me, or the ranch, or maybe Active Equipment, needs to pay the bill and make sure our insurance covers the liability." He switched his attention to the approaching bartender. "Can you give us two of those tall, frothy, orange things."

"You probably want to ask me tomorrow instead," said Danielle. "I've already had a couple of drinks, so I can't guarantee the quality of my advice."

He smiled at her. "Tomorrow's fine."

The bartender set the drinks on the bar top, and Travis handed him a tip.

"So, do you believe me now?" Travis asked as they turned away, heading in the general direction of the fountain pool.

"Believe you about what?"

"About Randal's motives."

"No," she answered with confidence.

Nothing had changed.

"He tried to hold your hand," Travis pointed out.

"He tried to get me away from you."

Travis took a sip of the drink and grimaced. Then he held it up to the light, inspecting it. "Really? *This* is what you're drinking."

"Cowboy up," she told him, using an expression she'd borrowed from Caleb.

"I think I'd rather come off a bucking bull."

"Wimp," she muttered.

"And why do you think he was so hell-bent on getting me away from you?" Travis asked.

"I don't know if you've noticed." They came to an empty bench facing the gardens, and she sat down. "But Randal doesn't like you much. And you're not helping matters by being so sarcastic all the time."

Travis sat down at the other end of the bench. "I don't know if *you've* noticed, but I'm not trying to make friends with Randal."

*"Really?"* she drawled with exaggerated sarcasm.

"I'm the competition, and he knows it."

"Oh, get over yourself."

"I kissed you, and he didn't."

"I used to date him, Travis." As soon as the words left her mouth, she regretted them.

Travis shifted on the bench. "I mean lately."

"Okay, no," she backpedaled. "He hasn't kissed me lately. Not in five years, as a matter of fact."

Travis took another, tentative sip of the drink, turning up his nose again. "Whereas, I kissed you last night. And he can tell it by my swagger."

"That's crazy." She tried for a haughty tone, but her words came out breathy as memories of the kiss bloomed in her mind.

Her body's reaction was nearly as strong as it had been in the garden, making her grateful to be in the middle of a crowd. Since, it was frighteningly tempting to do it again.

"What do you think he wanted to talk about?" Travis asked.

She pulled herself back from the unbidden fantasy. "He thinks I'm insulting Nester and Hedley by not snapping up their offer. He believes, and he's right, that they're the most prestigious law firm in D.C., and people would crawl over broken glass for the chance they're giving me."

"Doesn't mean it's right for you."

"Doesn't mean it's wrong."

Travis seemed to give that some thought. "Did he have anything to do with you getting the offer?"

"He says not." She took another drink.

"He also said he has a serious girlfriend."

"We have no evidence to suggest otherwise."

"Oh, yes, we do."

She pinned him with a dubious stare. "You are by far the most clairvoyant cowboy I have ever met."

"Doesn't take a mind reader to see what that guy's thinking."

Before she could respond, a neatly dressed waiter appeared in front of them. "Kobe beef sliders?" he asked, holding a silver tray out to Danielle.

"Yes, please," she answered, realizing she was

hungry. She helped herself to a cocktail napkin and one of the mini burgers.

Travis took two.

"If I don't eat something soon," said Danielle. "You'll have to pour me into bed."

The waiter quirked an amused smile as he backed away, and she realized how the words sounded.

She glanced at Travis. "I didn't mean…"

He grinned at her embarrassment. "I know what you meant."

A second waiter arrived, this one carrying a tray of champagne. At his offer, Danielle held up her half-full superior court and shook her head.

"Any chance I can exchange this for a beer?" Travis asked.

"Of course, sir." The waiter took his drink.

"Anything from DFB," said Travis.

"I'll be right back."

"You're very loyal," Danielle couldn't help but note as the waiter disappeared.

"Zach makes very good beer."

"Lots of companies make very good beer."

"Lots of companies aren't co-owned by my brother-in-law and the man who's engaged to my cousin."

"Unusually loyal," said Danielle, biting into the burger.

"And you're not?" asked Travis. "Don't they make lawyers take some kind of an oath?"

"That's confidentiality. And that's a professional relationship, not something lifelong like family."

Travis's tone turned curious. "What about your family?"

"What about them?"

"Are you close? You must be loyal to them." He examined one of the tiny burgers, biting off half.

"Loyal? Of course. Close? Well, we're not exactly that kind of family."

"What kind of family are you?"

"Just me and my parents."

"Are they lawyers?"

"They have law degrees, but they're corporate executives in New York City. Dad works in Midtown for a transportation conglomerate. Mom's downtown at an international fashion chain."

"Do you see them often?"

"Not really. We're not a, you know, Sunday dinner in the suburbs, confide your deepest secrets kind of family. We're all pretty self-sufficient."

He looked curious. "What does self-sufficient mean?"

She pondered how to elaborate. "You know how some mothers want their daughters to find a good man, get married and give them grandchildren?"

"I do," he nodded.

"My mother wasn't like that. She always told me not to count on a man to take care of me. It was vital that I educate myself, develop a good career. And if, *if* I decided to one day get married, it should be an equal partnership, with an iron-clad prenup to protect me when it all fell apart."

"That's not very romantic."

"Maybe not, but it is very practical." Danielle took another bite of the burger. "This is delicious."

"I was thinking cynical."

"Not delicious?" she joked.

"So, what would your mother think about Randal?"

"That I ought to be doubly careful with the prenup, since he's a smart attorney."

Travis smiled at that. "Maybe you should marry a dumb cowboy instead."

"Sure." She kept her tone deliberately light, memories of their kiss still doing a number on her hormones. "Know any?"

Travis laughed. "Was that an actual compliment?"

For a second she was puzzled.

"You don't think I'm dumb?" he prompted.

"I never thought you were dumb."

"Sure you did."

"I thought you were annoying."

"Your beer, sir." The waiter approached. "DFB C Mountain Ale."

"Perfect," said Travis, accepting the tall glass. "Thanks."

The waiter nodded and withdrew.

"Do you still think I'm annoying?" Travis asked, taking a swig.

"Sometimes," she admitted. Though those times were getting fewer and farther between. The Travis she was coming to know in Vegas wasn't like the one she remembered in Lyndon Valley.

"I'll try to do better," he offered.

"And here I thought you were *trying* to be annoying."

He gave a sheepish shrug. "Sometimes, I am. But only because I thought you were a snob."

"I'm not a snob," she told him with conviction. "I'm self-sufficient."

He thought about that for a moment. "I'm sorry about your family. They don't sound like much fun."

"They've been my family for a long time. I'm used to them." Though, for some reason, she found his sympathy touching.

His blue eyes were soft in the dim light, his expression uncharacteristically caring. He was handsome. He was sexy. He was smarter than she'd expected. And now he seemed genuinely compassionate.

She could feel herself being pulled to a very dangerous place. She struggled to remember all the reasons he irked her. He was a sarcastic, smart-ass, dusty, sweaty, tough-as-nails cowboy, who didn't have any use for big-city lawyers. He might kiss her, but he was never going to respect her as a person. If she let this thing go any further, she was definitely going to get hurt. Travis, on the other hand, would saunter away unscathed.

She forced herself to glance at her watch. "I think I'll call it a night."

"Had enough of lawyers?"

"Had one too many drinks." She rose to her feet. "These things are giving me a headache."

Travis rose with her. "Do you want me to walk you to the elevators?"

She quickly shook her head. "I'll be fine."

The last thing she was going to do was give herself a chance for second thoughts. She was walking away from Travis, his deep blue eyes, his strong, broad shoulders and his sexy smile, right this second. And she wasn't looking back.

# Five

Danielle made her way along a fieldstone walk-way that was illuminated by yellow-toned pot lights, past the lush gardens, the overhanging oak trees, and across a small footbridge that covered a babbling brook. She passed a few guests coming the other way, while the noise of the conference party gradually faded away behind her.

"Had enough?" Randal's voice unexpectedly broke the quiet as he came up beside her on the narrow path.

"Getting tired," she told him, deciding it was best to simply ignore their tiff from earlier.

"It was a good conference," he offered.

"Interesting discussions," she agreed. "I'm not

sure I concur with the direction the country seems to be taking on tariffs for emerging economies."

"You have to remove the exemption at some point," Randal countered. "Or you risk flooding the market and compromising domestic manufacturing."

"Maybe," she allowed. "But you also risk protectionism on the other side. Then again, I'm a little drunk, and so are you. This might not be the best time to make any sweeping policy decisions."

Randal laughed at that, sounding more like his old self, and she found herself relaxing.

"So, have you decided?" he asked.

"About moving to D.C.?"

"Yes, about moving to D.C. What else is there for you to decide?"

Whether or not to sleep with Travis was the first thing that came to Danielle's mind. But as quickly as the thought formed, she squelched it. She wasn't going to go there. There were less than two days until they went their separate ways, possibly for good. Once she was back in Chicago, and especially if she left there for D.C., she was certain these feelings would disappear.

"Danielle?" Randal prompted.

"I told them I'd let them know in a week."

He was silent, but she could feel his disapproval.

"It's the best I can do," she offered into the silence.

It was a great offer, but it was also a very big decision. Caleb Terrell wasn't the only client she'd miss working with. There were another half dozen that she'd represented for years. Their holdings were complex and interesting, and she liked to think she was a pivotal piece of their international successes so far.

"You're overthinking," said Randal, his voice tight.

The path widened out to a small, dim courtyard. A waterfall splashed at one side.

She stopped. She wasn't overthinking. She was thinking exactly the right amount, given the magnitude of the decision. And she wished he'd back off and let her do it.

"We can't keep having this same argument," she told him.

He gave her an easy smile. "We're lawyers. That's what we do."

"Well, I'm tired of doing it."

"Danielle." With a gentle hand on her shoulder, he urged her to one side of the courtyard.

She drew a deep sigh, but went along because she wanted to get this over with and get back to her room.

"Say whatever you need to say," she told him. "And then I'm going to bed."

His expression faltered for a second. But then it smoothed out. "Danielle." He took her hands in his.

She glanced down, uncomfortable with the intimacy of the gesture.

"I'm afraid if you leave here without deciding, you'll go back, get comfortable in Chicago, and you won't do what's best for you."

She raised her brows, looking at his face. "And you think you know what's best for me?"

"I know you pretty well," he countered.

"You once knew me pretty well," she corrected.

"I still do. People don't change that much." He paused, and his expression turned intense. "You and me…"

She was getting a bad feeling here. "You and me, what?"

His hands squeezed hers. "I can't help but wonder if we made a mistake. Moving to different cities, breaking things off, we never really—"

"Wait a minute." She tugged her hands from his. "You said you had a girlfriend."

"I do." He nodded rapidly. "I do. But, well, I'm not exactly sure where that's going."

"Don't do this, Randal. I'm not—"

He put an index finger across her lips. "Shh."

She was too shocked by his touch to react.

"Let it happen," he told her.

To her horror, he leaned in, tilting his head, closing his eyes, clearly intending to kiss her.

"Randal!" she squealed, quickly jumping back.

His eyes popped open and he stumbled.

"What do you think you're doing?" she demanded.

He rubbed his hand along her arm. "I'm showing you what can be."

"It can't be. It's not going to be."

"You can't possibly know that. We had something great once. If you take this job, if you come to D.C., we'll have a second chance."

She shook her head, moving farther back, and his hand dropped from her arm. "I'm not looking for a relationship, Randal."

"I'm not talking about two kids, a dog and a white picket fence. We can be good for each other. I can be great for your career."

She didn't deny that. Randal was a very successful lawyer, well respected in D.C. and across the country.

He stepped forward, expression softening, tone cajoling. "I'm not asking for a decision right this minute."

"I'm not going to mislead you, Randal. Yours isn't a direction I'm going in right now."

His features tightened. "So, *that* you can decide right here and right now?"

"Yes." She was positive she didn't want to rekindle something with Randal, surprisingly positive, in fact.

He frowned in annoyance. "It's him, isn't it?"

"Him, who? There is no him."

"The bull rider." There was venom in his tone. "You've got the hots for the bull rider."

"That's none of your business."

"That means yes."

She stepped away. "Good night, Randal."

"Danielle." His tone turned sweet as he took a step toward her.

"Don't." She held up her palms to stop him, continuing to walk backward. "You've had too much to drink. At least I hope you've had too much to drink. This isn't like you."

"Dani."

"No." She turned on her heel, walking swiftly down the path toward the hotel lobby.

There, she turned abruptly into the ladies' room, letting the door close behind her and dropping into a padded, French provincial chair in the entry area. She'd hide here for as long as it took, hours if necessary. But she wasn't going to risk running into Randal again.

Her mother had been right. And if it wasn't so late, Danielle might have been tempted to pick up a phone and tell her so. A woman couldn't trust any man to look out for her best interest. Men would always look out for their own.

Back-to-back with his paintball team member Reed Terrell, Travis gasped for breath. They were crouched behind a wooden barrier, having sprinted away from the "enemy." Both men were decked out in protective gear, and each held a paintball rifle filled with yellow balls. They'd split into three teams, blue, red and yellow. He and Reed were the last of the yellow team to still be "alive."

"How many do you think are out there?" Reed asked.

"Alex for sure on blue."

Reed coughed out a deep laugh. "Nobody wants to kill the groom."

Travis gripped his weapon. "I've got no problem killing the groom. But I think Caleb's still alive on red, and maybe Seth, too."

"I'll take out your brother, if you want to take out mine."

"I got Zach on the other side of the hill. So, I don't think there's anyone else besides Alex left on blue."

Something clanged against metal, and both men stilled.

"The shed," said Travis.

Reed peeked over the top of the wooden wall. "If we're fast, we can make the trench and follow it down to the hay bales."

"I'm fast," said Travis. "But you're more power than agility."

"You go first. I'll cover you, and maybe you'll get a shot."

"Unless he's inside the shed."

"Or maybe on the roof." Reed reached out and tapped Travis's shoulder, silently pointing upward.

Travis saw it, too. A slight movement at the peak of the roof. "Seth," he said.

"You sure?"

"Oh, yeah. He had that twisted gray thing on his helmet."

Reed peeked up again. "You can see from here?"

"Just a glimpse. But it's him."

Three rapid-fire shots echoed through the air, paintballs smacking against the wooden wall.

"They've found us," said Travis.

"Go for the trench."

Travis nodded. "On three."

Reed counted off. When he got to three, Travis sprinted out of their cover while Reed shot over his head.

He dove into the trench, quickly checking himself for paint splatters. He was unscathed.

He looked back and gave Reed a thumbs-up. Reed pointed toward the hill, and Travis quickly looked over, spotting Caleb. It took him a second to realize that Caleb was creeping up on Alex. He quickly signaled Reed to hold.

Caleb made it, stood up and fired once at Alex, hitting him in the back. Travis took three shots, hitting Caleb with two of them. Caleb turned in shock before going down on one knee. Travis quickly turned his attention to Seth.

It was obvious Seth knew somebody was in the trench, but he couldn't see Travis. He did, however, have a chance at hitting Reed. Travis bounced a shot off the near side of the roof and shouted for Reed to run. He shot again and again, hearing Reed's footsteps behind him.

Reed plunged into the trench beside him, breathing hard.

"Took out Caleb," said Travis.

"I saw that. Just Seth left?"

"I think so."

"I can almost taste the free beer," laughed Reed.

"He's got the high ground," Travis pointed out.

"Yeah, but he's practically a city slicker these days. And there are two of us. If we split up, the best he's going to do is take out one. Yellow team still wins."

"Good plan," Travis agreed.

"You go north along the hay bales," said Reed. "When you get to the far end, I'll run south over the field."

"That's suicide."

"Only if the city slicker can still shoot."

Travis grinned at the idea of Seth going soft. He couldn't imagine that ever happening.

"You're fastest," said Reed. "By the time he takes me out, you'll be around the end with a clear shot."

"Make sure you stay alive for at least twenty seconds."

"Will do," Reed said with a nod, adjusting his safety goggles.

"Good luck," said Travis.

"You, too."

Travis stealthily maneuvered his way along the trench, popping up behind the hay bales, then hugging them, crouched low, in an effort to get closer to the shed. When he came to the end of the bales, he turned to signal Reed.

With a mighty yell, Reed jumped up out of the

trench, dodging and weaving his way across the field, firing at the roof of the shed.

As soon as Seth started to shoot at Reed, Travis burst out from cover, sprinting as fast as he could around the end of the shed. He spotted Seth, stopped, breathed, put the rifle to his shoulder and squeezed off a careful shot.

He hit Seth square in the back, forcing a grunt and a cuss word from his lips. Travis grinned, while Reed whooped. The rest of the players cheered and whistled from the hillside.

While Seth made his way to the ladder, Reed appeared around the wall of the shed, grinning from ear to ear, holding up his arms and turning around to show Travis he hadn't been shot.

"City slicker jokes coming up," he gloated.

Travis held out his hand, giving Reed a firm shake. "Thanks, partner."

"Good shot," said Reed.

"He's a lot bigger than a gopher."

Reed laughed.

Seth hopped to the ground from the ladder and started toward them.

"Good day to be me," Reed joked.

"For the free beer?" Travis asked.

"And someone soft to sleep with. I'm the only one who brought his wife along."

"Katrina is here?" The revelation surprised Travis. He hadn't expected his sister to come along on a guys' weekend.

"When Caleb said he was meeting with Danielle, Katrina decided they should do some shopping."

"They're *together?*" Travis wasn't sure why the thought bothered him.

Reed looked at him strangely. "Yeah. Why? That a problem?"

"No, no. It's no problem."

Danielle and Katrina. Would Danielle mention their kiss? If she did, would Katrina tell Caleb? Would the whole valley end up knowing? Did he care?

"Travis?" asked Reed.

"Huh?"

"You fighting with Danielle again?"

"What fighting? We barely saw each other. She was hanging out with all those lawyers, and I was riding bulls and planning a bachelor party." He scoffed out a laugh. "Fighting. As if. We'd have to have been in the same room for more than a few minutes to be fighting."

"Travis?" Reed repeated.

"Yeah?" Travis struggled hard not to feel like a deer in the headlights.

"What the hell's wrong with you?"

\* \* \*

Katrina gazed fondly at the high-heeled, leopard-print pumps on her dainty feet. "I really don't need to buy another pair."

"Did you need to buy the last pair?" Danielle teased, gazing at the jeweled, gold sandals on her own feet.

Her freshly polished, glittering green-and-gold toenails peeked saucily up at her. It was an odd color, but Katrina had talked her into it during their pedicures. Now Danielle kind of liked it. And it certainly went with the shoes.

"I didn't actually need the last dozen pair," said Katrina, coming to her feet and moving to the mirror in the shoe store.

The saleswoman stood discreetly by, waiting to see if they needed assistance.

"They're gorgeous," said Danielle.

"They'd be great with jeans."

"Walk around on yours," Katrina urged.

Danielle stood. The shoes were surprisingly comfortable.

Katrina's enthusiasm ramped up. "We should go dancing tonight."

"Your husband is going to be busy at a kegger."

"Then tomorrow night," said Katrina. "We should stay an extra day."

"I can't," said Danielle. She'd already stretched out the trip way further than she'd planned.

"Sure, you can." Katrina waved away her refusal. "The Sasha Terrell Fund and Active Equipment are both very important clients."

"True enough," Danielle was forced to agree.

"If we want you to stay in Vegas to discuss, I don't know, spending strategies, you have to stay."

Danielle came to a stop in front of the mirror next to Katrina. *"Spending strategies?"*

"Yeah, you know, what to do with all our money and stuff."

"These really are killer shoes," said Danielle.

"That settles it. We're staying to dance."

"And Reed is going to agree to this?"

Katrina's lips curved into a suggestive smile. "I can get Reed to agree to anything."

"That's as much detail as I want to know."

Katrina gave a delighted laugh. "We're going to need dresses, something outrageously sparkly and short. The kind that make men's jaws drop open."

Danielle couldn't help but picture Travis's jaw dropping open. She tried to stop herself from thinking about him, but Katrina's carefree exuberance was infectious. It wasn't like anybody could read her mind. If she wanted to fantasize about gyrating on a dance floor in a short, sparkly dress and killer gold shoes in front of Travis, it was nobody's business but her own.

They bought the shoes. Then they made the rounds of some high-end dress shops, each laughing their way through about forty dresses. In the end, Katrina went with a mauve-and-white sheath, with a sparkling bodice and subtle, purple flowers on the skirt, saying that Reed liked her with a bit of color.

For Danielle, there was no choice but gold. She found a strapless party dress, with a glittering, tight bodice that fanned into a short, three layered, crinoline skirt, scattered with gold sequins. It was by far the sexiest thing she'd ever owned. She might have chickened out, but Katrina was very persuasive.

Purchases in hand, Katrina marched them straight to the nearest hotel, easily finding an available limo.

"Now, we're going to do something exciting," said Katrina as they pulled out from the entrance.

"This hasn't been exciting so far?"

It was one of Danielle's most indulgent days ever.

"Not yet," said Katrina with a secretive grin.

"I'm getting hungry." Danielle glanced at her watch, noticing it was after six.

"I have an appointment," said Katrina. Then she leaned forward to call to the driver. "Abyss Photo Studio, please."

"You need pictures?" Danielle wondered if they were for Katrina's dancing career.

"I need pictures," Katrina confirmed.

"In Vegas?" Surely, she got her publicity shots taken in New York.

"It's a special photographer that I heard about."

A few blocks down, they left the strip and pulled into a small parking lot in front of a neat, nondescript building.

"Would you like me to wait, ma'am?"

"That would be great," said Katrina, sliding forward to hand the man her credit card. "That way we can leave all the bags here. We might be an hour or more."

"Not a problem."

"An hour?" asked Danielle. "How many pictures do you need?"

"Quite a few." Katrina took back her card and bounced out of the limo.

Danielle followed. "These are for work?"

"Not work," said Katrina as she opened the shop door. "For Reed. He has a birthday coming up."

"Oh," Danielle responded politely as she followed her inside. But she was thinking Reed must have hundreds of pictures of Katrina.

Then she glanced around the opulent reception

area, taking in the sample pictures on the walls. *"Ohhh,"* she repeated. Now, she got it.

The portraits displayed were sensual, sexy, some of them downright erotic.

She followed Katrina to one of three private reception desks. "I guess Reed's going to be one happy birthday boy."

"I hope so," said Katrina. "What he really wants is a baby."

Danielle couldn't help but be surprised. "You're thinking about getting pregnant?"

"Not right now. Maybe in a couple of years."

"Would you have to give up dancing?"

"I'll want to retire from the stage eventually, maybe do choreography, or something else behind the scenes. When your husband donates ten million dollars to your ballet company, you can pretty much have any job you want."

"Is that the trick to unfettered employability?" Danielle joked. She'd been helping Reed and Katrina manage the Sasha Terrell Fund, named after Reed's mother, for nearly two years now.

Katrina gave her an answering smile. Then she sat down in an armchair in front of a neatly dressed, friendly looking woman. "Katrina Terrell. I have an appointment."

Danielle took the chair beside her.

The woman smiled brightly at both of them. "Will we be taking your pictures together?"

Katrina drew back in obvious confusion. Then she glanced at Danielle and her eyes danced with amusement. "Oh, no, we're just friends."

Danielle stifled a grin. "I'm only here for moral support."

The woman was obviously embarrassed. "I'm so sorry. I misunderstood."

Katrina waved the apology away. "No problem. If I was going to have a girlfriend, it would be Danielle."

Danielle's grin grew wider. "Thanks. I think."

Katrina twisted her body, giving Danielle a considering look. "You know…"

"I don't think Reed would let me date you," Danielle gamely carried on the joke.

"That's not what I was thinking."

"Good to hear."

"I was thinking you should get some pictures done, too." Katrina quickly turned back to the woman. "Do you have time to give us each a photo shoot?"

Danielle felt her jaw go lax. "I'm not—"

"Certainly," the woman agreed, typing into her computer. "We can manage that."

"Oh, no," Danielle stated with conviction.

"Oh, yes," said Katrina, nodding happily.

"I don't even have a boyfriend."

"You will someday. Save them. Put them away."

"I'm not dressing up like a floozy. What if they end up on the internet?"

"There's no chance of that," said the woman. "We give you a glossy copy of your favorite shots, and you keep the original memory card. We don't keep a single record here."

"Come on," Katrina cajoled. "It'll be a blast."

"I'm way too shy," Danielle protested.

"You are not. Besides, they can be romantic. They don't have to be naughty."

"This is ridiculous," said Danielle.

Maybe if she had someone to surprise. Maybe if she had…

Her brain flashed an image of Travis, but she determinedly shook it away.

"You're not getting any younger," said Katrina.

"Excuse me?"

"You'll have a boyfriend again. Of course you'll have a boyfriend again. And probably soon. And if it's not soon, and if you're getting kind of old and wrinkly, I bet he'll want to see pictures of you when you were young and hot."

"I'm not getting old that fast." Then again, would

she want to do this when she was older? Not that she was saying she wanted to do it now.

"When are you going to have a chance like this again?" asked Katrina.

"Our photographers are the top of their field," noted the woman behind the desk. "The pictures can be very tasteful. You pick the costumes yourself. And each customer can choose four pieces of lingerie that are yours to keep. We have the latest and most luxurious lines."

"My treat," said Katrina, handing the woman her credit card.

"Really, I can't," said Danielle.

The woman accepted the credit card. "We have an extraordinarily high level of customer satisfaction."

"Ring it through," urged Katrina.

"Do you have anything in flannel?" asked Danielle.

"No, but we have some full-length, satin nighties. I tell you what," said the woman, swiping Katrina's card. "If you're not completely satisfied, we'll destroy the memory card and I'll refund Mrs. Terrell's money."

Danielle couldn't quite find an argument for that, and she found herself agreeing.

In the end, she had an astonishingly good time.

They started with a makeup artist and a hairdresser, before moving into the clothing store.

The studio provided complimentary champagne, which they drank while joking their way through lacy baby-dolls, slips and camisoles. Katrina braved a low-cut, black push-up bra and a pair of tiny panties. In the end, Danielle threw caution to the wind and modeled a magenta teddy, with gold, satin trim and mesh cut-outs across her middle. She paired it with black stockings and her new jeweled shoes.

"We have *got* to find you a boyfriend," said Katrina as they gazed at the photo proofs, selecting ten for immediate printout.

Danielle hesitated over one of the magenta teddy pictures. She was turned slightly to one side, her hair looking soft and sexy, her eyes bright, smile provocative, the angle hinting at the curve of her hip and her behind.

Katrina nudged her in the arm. "Don't be so shy. The camera loves you. I sometimes wear less than that when I dance."

"You're the one the camera loves," said Danielle, switching her attention to the pictures of Katrina. There was a reason audiences adored her as a prima ballerina.

"We're both pretty hot."

Though Danielle might be reluctant to admit

it, she was surprisingly happy with the pictures. The photographer had known just how to capture her best looks. The lighting was soft, and her skin seemed to glow.

Katrina took over the mouse and dragged the magenta teddy shot into Danielle's print basket. "There, that's ten."

"I can't believe that's me," Danielle admitted.

"Well, I sure can." Katrina straightened. "Let's go find ourselves some dinner."

The photographer packaged their prints and handed each of them their memory cards. Danielle secured everything in her shoulder bag, and they headed back to the limo.

After a fabulous dinner, and a late night of girl talk with Katrina, the limo driver pulled up to the front doors of the Emperor Plaza.

"Don't worry about the bags, ma'am," the driver instructed as he helped Katrina out of the car.

"Welcome back," greeted a uniformed porter, smiling at both women. "We'll be happy to deliver your packages."

"Room thirty-four sixteen," said Katrina.

"And your name, ma'am?"

"Katrina Terrell." She pointed. "Those five are mine. The others can go to Danielle Marin's room."

"Eighteen twenty-two," Danielle added.

"We'll take care of it. Have a good night, ladies."

They thanked the limo driver and made their way into the brightly lit lobby.

"They're in the Ace High Lounge," said Katrina.

"Who?"

"Reed and the rest of the guys."

"You're not going near that place, are you?" Danielle had no desire to go anywhere near a bachelor party at midnight.

"It's my husband, my brother-in-law and two brothers."

"And thirty-five other men."

"Who won't dare look at us sideways."

"What do you mean us?"

"Come on." Katrina studied a brass sign. She pointed down a hallway. "This way."

"I'm tired," Danielle protested. She was. "I want to go to bed."

Katrina linked her arm and tugged her forward. "Too bad. You have to come and keep me company."

"Who says?"

"I say. And I just paid for your sexy pictures."

"I thought we agreed never to speak of them again." Danielle wanted to get them safely locked away as soon as possible. She was beginning to worry about carrying them through airport security. What if someone searched her luggage? How embarrassing would that be?

Katrina laughed, still tugging her along the hallway. "Your secret's safe with me. Come on. You owe me."

"I paid for dinner," Danielle pointed out, but she gave up and kept walking.

"Aren't you at all curious?"

"About what men do at bachelor parties?" asked Danielle. "I honestly don't want to know."

"Maybe someone jumped out of a cake."

"I hope not. That's so eighties."

"I'm sure they kept it tasteful."

"Travis did the planning."

"Good point. This might be more exciting than I thought. Here we are."

Danielle hesitated. If it turned out there were strippers in there, it was going to be mortifiying.

Before they could pull on the door, it opened from the inside, loud music thumping from the depths of the dim room. Caleb appeared, jerking back in obvious surprise at the sight of them.

"Katrina. Danielle." He gave a wide grin. "What are you guys doing here?" It was subtle, but his speech was measured, as if he was being careful to properly enunciate his words.

The door swung shut behind him.

"Having a good party?" asked Katrina.

"Fantastic," he responded. "You want me to get Reed?"

"We want to find out what's going on inside," said Katrina.

"No, we don't," said Danielle.

"You always were the smart one," Caleb said to Danielle.

"Thank you."

"What's going on in there?" asked Katrina.

"We're drinking DFB beer and watching a game."

"Are you drunk?" asked Katrina.

"I am not."

"Is Reed drunk?"

"Reed doesn't get drunk."

The door opened again, bashing into Caleb's shoulder and sending him stumbling.

This time, it was Travis who appeared.

"Danielle," he grinned heartily. "You're back."

"We've been shopping," said Katrina.

"So, I heard, baby sister."

"And out for dinner," she continued.

Danielle held her breath, fearing Katrina might mention the pictures. But the door opened again, and Reed joined them.

He zeroed in on Katrina. "Hey, sweetheart." He

moved to stand next to her, putting a hand on the small of her back and giving her a quick kiss on the temple. "Did you have a good time?"

"It was great. I got you a birthday present."

Danielle stilled, bracing herself. She couldn't help a fleeting glance at Travis, and found herself shifting from one foot to the other.

"What did you get me?" asked Reed.

"Oh, no," Katrina teased, waggling a finger. "Not until your birthday."

"Yeah?" he growled on a challenging note.

"Yeah," she responded saucily.

"We'll see about that." He looped an arm around her shoulders. "Good night, boys," he called to Travis and Caleb, as he steered her down the hall.

Their departure spurred Danielle to action. "I'll say good-night as well," she told Caleb, glancing briefly to Travis as she backed away.

"We can talk tomorrow," said Caleb.

The words brought Danielle to a halt. "Were you looking for me today?"

She and Caleb had met briefly when he arrived Thursday night. But she'd understood he was going to be busy all day. At least that's what Katrina told her. Now she realized she'd never actually checked with Caleb.

Caleb shook his head. "I'd have called you. To-morrow's fine."

"Okay," Danielle nodded, relieved. "I'll be there."

"I'm done, too," said Travis, breaking away from his brother, and coming up next to Danielle.

Her stomach gave an involuntary quiver of excitement.

Caleb glanced back at the closed door. "Yeah," he agreed. "I think the party's winding down." He started forward.

Reed and Katrina were far ahead in the lobby, disappearing around the central fountain.

"Thanks for entertaining Katrina," said Caleb. "I know Reed appreciates it."

Danielle gave a short laugh. "Katrina entertained me. I feel like I've been playing hooky all day long."

"You put in way too many hours," said Caleb.

"A lot of lawyers put in more hours than I do."

She couldn't help thinking about Randal and the others at Nester and Hedley. How hard did they work? What was the pace like in D.C.?

"I'm in the north tower," said Caleb, pointing to an elevator sign, and turning toward the hallway. "'Night."

"Good night," Danielle called after him.

She and Travis walked a few feet in silence.

"I'm west," she told him.

"I know."

She remembered he'd walked her to the elevators that first night.

"How was the bachelor day?" she asked.

"No insurance claims from the dune buggy races," he said, reminding her of the policy she'd reviewed for him yesterday.

"That's good news. Who won?"

"Alex."

Danielle gave him a suspicious look. "The groom? Was the fix in?"

"Maybe a little. Reed and I rocked at paintball. We took it for the yellow team."

Danielle couldn't help but smile at the pride in his voice. "First the bull riding, and now paintball. There's just no stopping you, is there?"

"No, ma'am, there is not." There was a wry note in his voice, as he reached out to press the call button for the west tower elevators.

Two older women joined them waiting.

"You don't need to wait for the car," said Danielle. "My suite's up there, too."

# Six

The middle elevator car pinged, the red up arrow lighting. Three men strode with them into the elevator, along with the two older ladies. Danielle pressed eighteen and moved into a corner, while Travis pressed thirty-four, the top floor, and shifted to stand beside her.

One of the three men took a lingering, visual tour of her white slacks and blue tank top. She ignored him, but Travis stepped in front of her, lifting his chin and folding his arms across his chest.

She couldn't help but smile at the gesture. For some reason it sent a shot of warmth through her chest. It was gentlemanly, she told herself, kind of sweetly old-fashioned.

The men filed out on the fourteenth floor, and she stepped out from behind Travis, smiling and shaking her head. "You didn't have to—" As she moved farther, her shoulder bag snagged on the elevator rail, jerking out of her hand, clattering upside down to the floor.

Danielle swore. Travis turned at the sound. And the two older ladies stared at the items bouncing on the floor.

Travis crouched to help, while Danielle scooped up her wallet and cell phone, snagged a makeup bag, her keys and a hand mirror. She stuffed them into the open bag, checking the floor to make sure nothing more embarrassing had slipped out.

Then she realized Travis had gone still. She twisted her neck to look at him, freezing in horror when she saw the envelope in his hands. Her boudoir photos had fallen halfway out, and he was staring, eyes wide, at the magenta teddy photo on the top of the stack.

He rose, silently sliding the photos back into the envelope and refolding the flap.

Danielle couldn't speak. She couldn't look at him. The embarrassing shot scuttled through her brain. It was her worst nightmare come true.

He handed her the envelope as the elevator pinged

on the eighteenth floor. But, before she could exit, his hand wrapped around her upper arm.

The women glanced at her in puzzlement.

His grip wasn't tight. She could have easily pulled away, darted for the door, escaped and left town, finding a way to never, ever face him again.

But she didn't. She complied with his unspoken request.

The door slid shut, and the elevator rose.

While they moved, Danielle turned hot, then cold, then hot again.

The doors opened on twenty-three, and the two women got off. Travis kept hold of her arm. He stayed silent until the doors had shut completely.

When he spoke, his voice was guttural. "Tell me they're not for Randal."

The question surprised her so much, she forgot to answer.

"Tell me," he repeated with an edge of desperation.

"They're not for Randal," she quickly told him. "They're not for anybody. They were a lark, a silly, stupid idea that I regret already."

He nodded sharply. His hand slipped from her arm. "Okay."

That was it? One word? What did he mean?

The elevator pinged on thirty-four, the doors opening yet again.

Travis crossed the car. He pressed eighteen again then moved through the doorway.

Danielle's knees went weak with relief, or maybe it was disappointment. She couldn't quite pinpoint which.

But then he stopped. The doors started to shut, but he stuck his arm out to block them. He turned fully around, gaze intense, seeming to drink in the sight of her and swallow it whole.

"I've tried so damn hard to ignore this," he rasped.

Heat and desire washed over her again. She told herself to shut up. She told herself to stay still and let it pass.

"So have I," she confessed in a small voice.

He didn't move. He waited.

Her stomach contracted. Her blood pounded in her ears. She struggled to suck in oxygen.

*Stay put,* her logical brain ordered.

There was absolutely no mistaking the hunger in his expression. His eyes were dark, his jaw clenched tight. His entire body seemed poised to pounce.

If she moved, she was done for. They were done for. If she took one step toward him, she'd be in his bed in minutes. And nothing would ever be the same between them again.

She moved one foot, and then the other. In seconds, she was out the door and into the hallway.

He turned beside her, released the door, silently took her hand in his and made his way along the short hallway.

Neither spoke as he swiped his key card in the double doors at the end. One door swung open, soft music greeting them, warm air, thick carpets, soft lighting, scented oil wafting through a richly appointed living room.

They walked inside, and the door clicked shut behind them. Astonishingly, her trepidation disappeared. Her uncertainty and fear vanished. She knew she was right where she wanted to be. She was alone with Travis at last, and all the reasons to keep her distance seemed to evaporate into thin air.

He turned to face her, his own expression relaxing. He smiled gently, blue eyes softening in the dim light. He smoothed back her hair. And with the opposite hand, he twined their fingers together.

"You are so incredibly beautiful," he whispered.

"How did this happen?" she breathed, wondering if this might be a dream.

"My guess is good genes and healthy living."

She couldn't help but smile.

His own smile faded, his gaze zeroing in on her lips, his hand moving to cradle her cheek.

"I'm about to kiss you," he warned.

"I'm about to kiss you back."

"You promise?"

"I promise."

He leaned in, voice deep and low. "This is going to be fun."

Her laughter was quickly lost in the touch of his lips. They were smooth, firm and hot. He smelled of male musk, tasted of smoky scotch whiskey. He deepened the kiss, and she welcomed him in.

He wrapped his arm around the small of her back, pulling her against him. Her bag dropped to the floor as she reveled in the heat of his steel hard thighs. She wrapped her arms around his neck, letting her head fall back, drinking in the magic of his kiss and letting waves of passion wash through her.

His thumb slipped beneath the hem of her tank top, stroking the bare skin of her back, tracing the small bumps of her spine, first up and then down.

Feeling her way, she flicked open the buttons of his shirt, sliding her palms along his washboard stomach and the definition of his chest, eliciting a groan from deep in his throat. She found a small scar near his left nipple, tracing the ridge with her fingertip. She eased back from his kiss, dipping her head to kiss the scar. Then she kissed a path to his shoulder, pushing off his shirt.

He shrugged out of it, finding her lips, kissing her deeply as his hands skimmed her bare skin and cupped her breasts through her lacy bra. He groaned again and scooped her into his strong arms. She clung to him, still kissing as he carried her across the suite, through a set of double doors, and into a massive bedroom with a four-poster bed.

The room was lit softly by a bedside lamp. The French doors were propped open, sheer curtains billowing in the warm breeze.

He set her on her feet. Then he peeled off her tank top, pulling it over her raised arms, tossing it on a nearby chair while his gaze feasted on her snowy white bra.

"You get more beautiful by the second."

She splayed her hands across his tanned chest. "So do you." She found the scar again. "Bull?" she asked.

"Don't remember."

"Seriously?"

"I've got a few of them. Does it bother you?"

"Not at all. They make you seem rugged and sexy."

He gave a playful grin. "I am rugged and sexy."

"That you are," she agreed. Then, feeling bold, she reached back and released her bra, letting it fall away. "I'm not exactly rugged."

He drank in the sight of her bare breasts. "I'd hate it if you were. You're soft and sexy, exactly how you're supposed to be."

She watched as his tanned, callused hand closed over her breast. His palm was warm, but her nipple beaded hard in reaction.

He curled an arm around her waist again, drawing her close.

"Soft," he whispered as his lips came down on hers.

She inhaled his scent, drank in his taste, tangled her tongue with his. He felt so incredibly good pressed against her. She gave her passion free rein, letting the rest of the world fall away.

He seemed content to kiss her forever. But the heat was building inside her, and she was impatient to feel all of him. She slipped her hand between their bodies, popping the button on the top of his jeans.

He copied her move, releasing her button.

She slid down his zipper.

He sucked in a breath, and did the same.

She pulled back and smiled. Stepping away, she kicked off her shoes and shimmied out of her jeans.

He did the same, standing in black boxers, staring at her skimpy, white lace panties.

She hooked her thumbs into the thin strip of fabric.

He snagged his waistband.

"Shall we count to three?" she joked.

"Three." He stripped down his boxers, kicking them across the floor.

She waited, just to see what he'd do.

He crossed the small space and drew her into his arms. His hands skimmed down her back, cupping her buttocks while he kissed her neck. His magical lips made their way to her shoulder, across her chest. Then with excruciating slowness drew one nipple into his hot mouth.

She groaned with pleasure, scraping her fingernails across his thick hair. He moved to the other, and she gripped his shoulders to steady herself. A craving pushed its way through her bloodstream, peaking her nipples and pooling in her lower belly.

She gasped his name.

He instantly scooped her up, lifting her to lay her on the soft, satin bed. He reached for her panties, drawing them slowly down the length of her legs. Then he rose above her, all sinew, strength and power. It was by far the sexiest moment of her life.

Without hesitating, she eased her legs apart.

"More beautiful by the second," he rasped, bending lower to kiss the inside of her knee.

As he worked his way up, she couldn't hold still, twitching then squirming, then gasping and arching off the bed as he reached home. He kept going, kissing her belly, making her quiver as he reached her breasts, then her neck, then finally her mouth.

She slid her hands down his back, over his buttocks, around to grasp him, reveling in the hot texture and her own anticipation.

"You in a hurry?" he rasped in her ear.

"Yes," she hissed. "Yes, yes, yes."

He reached for the bed stand, producing a condom.

In moments, he was above her again, kissing her deeply, kneading her bottom, adjusting her thighs, pressing against her, slipping inside her, deeper and deeper. He felt so incredibly good.

She groaned in satisfaction, tipping her hips, wrapping her legs around him. His tongue stroked the inside of her mouth. Her hands gripped his back, tighter and tighter. Desire coiled in her belly, while his long strokes and satisfying rhythm spiraled her higher and higher.

The room grew hotter, and moisture beaded across her body. Traffic sounds blended to a roar in her ears, while the breeze teased her damp, sensitized skin. Then time and space disappeared, nothing existing except the pulse of Travis and the primal urge of her own body to reach for the pinnacle of release.

Color glowed to life inside her brain, shooting sparks of light along her synapses while pleasure built along her limbs, curling her toes and drawing moans of intense desire from her deep in her chest. Travis echoed the sounds, increasing his pace, his breathing speeding up, his heart thumping strong against her chest.

Then, her body roared and her world convulsed, and she cried out his name while waves of pure pleasure raced through her body. His kiss deepened, and he grasped her tightly to him while his own body shuddered with completion.

She spent long minutes drawing in deep breaths, her chest moving up and down. He shifted his weight, easing partway off, one leg staying over hers, his hand splayed across her stomach. The ornate, white pine posts of the bed came into focus, then the paintings on the wall, mounted above a cream-colored sofa and two peach armchairs.

She pushed her damp hair back from her forehead and stretched the kinks out of her legs. "Probably a good thing we didn't know that."

He kissed the tip of her shoulder. "Didn't know what?"

She turned to look at him, not feeling remotely

coy or shy. "How it would be between us. We might not have waited two years."

Comprehension dawned in his eyes, and his mouth crooked in a wry smile. "I might not have waited two minutes."

The first thing to enter Travis's sleep-filled brain was the scent of wild flowers. His thoughts wafted to Lyndon Valley, the springtime colors, the rolling hills. But then he felt the satin skin of Danielle's stomach, warm and soft under his rough fingertips. He heard her breathing and realized the scent was her shampoo.

This was better than home, so much better than home.

He blinked his eyes open to gaze at her delicate profile. Her hair was mussed from sleep, her eye makeup slightly smeared, her cheeks flushed, and her dark lips parted.

She'd stayed.

He smiled at the knowledge that she'd slept in his arms.

"You're awake early," came her husky voice.

"So are you," he whispered in return.

"You woke me up."

"I didn't mean to."

"You moved your leg."

"I didn't mean to do that, either." He'd have stayed perfectly still for hours if it kept her in his arms.

She stifled a yawn with the back of her hand, opening her dark fringed, coffee-brown eyes to look at him. "What time is it?"

"I don't know. Maybe seven."

She shifted up on one elbow, the drape of the white sheet covering her rounded breasts. "Do you have to get up?"

"Not yet. You?"

She shook her head. "I need to meet with Caleb, but my flight's not until noon." Then her expression faltered, and she sat up, bringing the sheet with her. "Unless you want me to have to get up. I can't tell, was that a question or a hint?"

He reached out to slide an arm around her waist, tugging her back toward him. "It was definitely a question. And I was absolutely hoping you'd say no."

He stretched up to meet her, kissing her lips.

He'd meant it to be playful, but the kiss quickly deepened to sensual. She kissed him back, and it turned very serious. Arousal instantly snaked its way through his body. He eased back on the pillow, drawing her against his bare chest.

His hands stroked down her back, reminding himself of every inch of her. She stretched out, lay-ing on top of him, limbs entwining with his, her soft breasts pressing against his chest. His arms wrapped themselves around her, holding her close, losing himself in the magic of her taste, scent and texture.

She drew back, smiling. "Good morning."

"Good morning," he responded, trying to gauge if he was taking things too fast.

"I forgot to tell you something."

Disappointment slid through him. "You have to go?"

"No. Not that." She pushed up so that she was sitting, straddling his hips.

He liked that position, liked it a lot, even though the moist contact of her body made it difficult to concentrate on anything she might say. He struggled not to fix his gaze on her beautiful breasts. They were round, pert, beautifully pink-tipped, and exactly the right size for his palm.

"Randal tried to kiss me."

Travis's attention flew to her face.

"He *what?*"

"He tried to kiss me. After the windup reception."

"Did you let him?"

Though Travis knew leaping from the bed to slam a fist into Randal's face was stupid—for one thing,

Randal was back in D.C.—he desperately wanted to injure the man.

"No, I didn't let him," Danielle responded tartly.

Travis felt marginally better. "What happened?"

"He tried to talk me into accepting the job in D.C. He said he didn't know where things were going with his girlfriend. And this would give us a second chance."

Travis battled hard against the anger and frustration building inside him. He wasn't angry with Danielle. It wasn't her fault Randal had no morals. Still, his tone came out harsher than he'd intended. "Do you want a second chance?"

She glanced down at their naked bodies. "Do I *look* like I want a second chance with Randal?"

Good point. She was in Travis's bed, naked, and Randal was halfway across the country. Some of his anger dissipated.

"What I'm saying here, is that you were right, and I was wrong. I misjudged Randal. I'm owning up to that."

Travis's hands reflexively reached forward, bracketing her hips, hoping he'd heard what he thought he'd heard. "What did you just say?"

"You want me to repeat it?"

His body felt lighter, a smile tugging at his lips. "Yeah."

"Okay, Travis Jacobs. You were right, and I was wrong."

"Will you marry me?"

The second the words were out, a wave of emotion cascaded through his body. He wasn't sure whether it was horror, shock or longing. He did know it had been a dumb thing to say, even as a joke.

Luckily, Danielle laughed. "Sorry, Travis. But your ego is going to have to make it through life without my constant reinforcement."

He gave an exaggerated sigh of disappointment.

"So, what are you going to do?" he asked.

She sobered. "I'm still thinking about it. If I go to D.C., Randal might be a hassle for a while. But he'll eventually get the message."

Travis hoped that was the case. He hated the thought that Randal might somehow change her mind.

"It's a fantastic opportunity," she told him wistfully.

Travis found his focus going to his hands. They were calloused and scarred, tanned dark against her creamy, soft skin. There was no better metaphor for the distance between them.

He might want her. He certainly wanted her badly at the moment. But the divide between them was huge. He was a coarse, backwoods cowboy, who made a living with his hands. She was a gorgeous, sophisticated woman, brilliant enough to take on the best in the world and win.

Unexpectedly, her fingertips touched against his stomach. "What about you?" she asked.

He didn't understand the question, so he made a joke. "Nobody offered me a job in D.C."

"Have you ever thought about what you want to do?"

"I'm a Colorado rancher."

"I know that. But you hinted that night at the party that you might have broader aspirations. Your brother and sisters all expanded their horizons."

Travis tried not to be offended by her phrasing. "Corey thinks I should go pro on the bull riding circuit."

"Wow." She squeezed her hands around his waist. "That'll challenge your intellect."

His jaw tensed. "We can't all be geniuses."

"I'm sorry," she offered.

"Sorry that I'm not a genius?"

She smacked his hip with her open palm. "Sorry that you're such a grouch."

He gave her a suggestive wag of his brow. "Want to do that again?"

She tossed her short hair. "You're trying to distract me."

"I'm glad you're catching on."

"You don't want to talk about it, do you?"

He pulled into a sitting position, bringing his face in front of hers. "Talking is definitely *not* what I want to do right now."

She looped her arms over his shoulders. "What is it you want to do, cowboy?"

He lifted his brow again. "Can I see the rest of your pictures?"

The question clearly took her by surprise. "I'm burning those damn pictures."

He smoothed back her hair, tone cajoling. "Oh, don't do that. Lock them away if you want to, but don't destroy them."

"It was a foolish idea to have them taken. I'm not the kind of woman who takes naughty pictures."

He slipped his hands up her hips, along her waistline and over the sides of her breasts. He cradled her face. "I happen to like the Danielle who takes naughty pictures."

She hissed in a tight breath. "What happens in Vegas, should definitely stay there."

He gave her a brief, gentle kiss, telling himself to keep a rein on his passion. Whatever they did next, was up to her.

"What else do you want to happen in Vegas?" he asked.

Her shoulders relaxed. "We're going to do it again, aren't we?"

He kissed his way along her shoulder. "Doing it again has my vote."

"You're incorrigible."

He smiled at that.

"Then again, I seem to be incorrigible too."

"That's a fair division of incorrigibility," he noted.

Her arms tightened around his neck, and her soft body melted against him. "You are an exceedingly sexy, handsome, exciting man."

"And you are the woman of my dreams." He kissed her deeply, giving his burgeoning passion free rein and letting his hands roam.

She moaned against his mouth, her nipples beading against his chest, heat and moisture gathering where their bodies met. Her kisses were the sweetest thing in the world. And her soft, smooth body seemed custom-designed for his.

Once again, he let the world disappear, immersing himself in Danielle, determined this time to make their lovemaking last for hours.

Wrapped in a fluffy, white, hotel bathrobe and curled up in a padded lounger on Travis's hotel suite balcony, Danielle sipped a strong cup of coffee. She was fresh from the shower, and the midmorning air was cool against her scalp.

Travis appeared in the open doorway clutching a mug of coffee. A pair of navy sweats rode low on his hips. His chest was bare. He was now clean-shaven, and his hair was also damp. She tried not to stare, but she couldn't help marveling at his rugged sex appeal. She'd spent half of last night and most of this morning making love with him, but she'd jump into bed again if he so much as crooked his little finger.

There had to be something wrong with her.

Her phone pinged and vibrated on the small, metal table next to her lounger.

"The real world?" Travis asked, moving to the second lounger.

"Seems like." She smiled at him, reaching for the phone.

He eased his body into the lounger, lifting his bare feet while the sun rays gleamed against his tanned chest.

Gaze hopelessly glued to his sinewy body, Danielle pressed the answer button and put her phone to her ear.

"Hello?"

"Hey, Danielle. It's Caleb."

"Morning, Caleb." She met Travis's eyes.

"Are you up and around?"

"I just showered," she answered.

Travis grinned at the way she used the truth.

"I'm meeting Reed and Katrina for breakfast in the Garden Café. Can you join us?"

"Of course." She guiltily reminded herself she was supposed to be here on business.

"Twenty minutes?"

"I'll be there."

"Great." Caleb signed off.

She let her phone drop into her lap. "Duty calls," she told Travis, trying not to feel dejected by the need for such an abrupt departure.

Their interlude was never going to be anything but temporary. It was over, and that was that. She'd have to go directly from breakfast to the airport, and she might not see Travis again for months. If she took the job in D.C., months might turn into forever.

For a split second the thought of never seeing Travis again made her panic.

His phone chimed, and he scooped it from the table as she stood up.

"Yeah?" He paused. "Hey, Caleb."

She stilled, locking gazes with Travis.

"Breakfast?" he asked into the phone. "Sure. When?"

There was another pause. "I'll be there," he said and hung up.

Danielle hesitated. She felt a ridiculous sense of relief that she didn't have to walk away from Travis this very minute. But they were going to breakfast with his friends and family. They likely wouldn't have a chance to say a personal goodbye. She wasn't sure what to do.

Travis stood. His expression was serious as he moved the few steps to stand in front of her.

"Kiss me goodbye?" he asked, gently sliding his hand around the back of her neck.

"I don't know what to say," she confessed. It seemed to be suddenly ending so fast.

"I don't, either," he told her, easing forward.

His free arm went around her waist, pressing her to his body. His lips touched hers, gently, softly, far too fleetingly.

He drew back, voice a whisper. "You surprised me, Danielle Marin."

"You surprised me right back," she admitted. In a few short days, Travis had turned her opinion of him on its ear.

"Are we going to leave this all in Vegas?" he asked.

"I don't see that we have any choice." But an unexplainable pain pressed into the center of her chest.

"You're right," he sighed.

Then he placed a soft kiss at her hairline, then his lips moved against her skin as he spoke. "When I wave an impersonal goodbye to you in the lobby later on? Know that what I really mean is this."

He bent his head, tilting sideways, kissing her long and hard and deep.

It ended far too soon.

"I'll mean that, too," she managed.

"Okay." He nodded and took a step back. "Okay."

She put a steadying hand on the doorjamb, ordering herself to move back inside the suite. "I'll go down to my room and change."

"I'll meet you in the café."

"In the café," she agreed, allowing herself a long, final look.

# Seven

Caleb was alone when Danielle approached the table. It was large and round, set in one corner of the second floor patio, overlooking the pool.

"'Morning," Caleb greeted, rising and pulling out the chair next to him.

"How are you feeling?" She couldn't help remembering how jovial he'd been at the end of the party last night.

"None the worse for wear. Did you have fun with Katrina?"

Shopping and dinner with Katrina seemed like a long time ago. "We had a great time."

"Good. The bachelor party went well. But I think Alex is getting pretty sick of all this guy stuff and about ready to get married now."

Danielle laughed at that as she sat down.

"I had a call from a Pantara executive last week," said Caleb, taking his own seat.

"Pantara Tractors?" Danielle named a huge, European equipment supplier, headquartered in Germany.

Caleb nodded. "They're interested in a merger."

The announcement surprised her, since Pantara was nearly twice the size of Active Equipment. "With you?" she confirmed.

"Yes, with me."

"They want to merge or buy you out?" She certainly wouldn't recommend Caleb sell to the competition.

"Merge. I'd remain CEO, with a voting majority, and we'd create a new class of preferred shares."

She sat back in her chair, puzzled at the apparent generosity of the offer. "Why?"

"That's what I need *you* to find out."

"So, there really was a legitimate reason for me to stay in Vegas."

He gave a mock expression of astonishment. "Of course there was a legitimate reason. What made you think there wasn't?"

"Well, I haven't done much work since you got here."

"That's about to change."

"'Morning," came Travis's gravelly voice.

She reflexively glanced up, and a wave of familiar warmth flowed through her body at the sight of him. "'Morning," she responded, her tone more husky than she'd intended.

Travis, on the other hand, kept his expression perfectly impassive as he gave her a passing smile. She felt half-dejected, half-impressed.

"Hungover?" Caleb asked him.

"Me?" Travis took a chair across the round table. "I was pacing myself. Zach's the one we should worry about."

Danielle couldn't help wishing Travis could sit next to her, but she understood why he couldn't.

"Zach's been a party animal all his life," said Caleb. "He'll be fine."

"Have you ordered?" asked Travis.

"Nope," Caleb answered. "I was just talking to Danielle about being my point person for the Pantara merger."

"Is that going to work out for her?" Travis snagged Danielle's gaze, and she realized he had to be wondering about the impact of the Nester and Hedley offer.

She could tell by his expression that he thought she should tell Caleb about her possible job change. And he was absolutely right about that. She owed it to Caleb to be honest. If she might not be around for the Pantara deal, he needed to know now.

"Caleb?" She angled her body to face him.

"Hmm?" He'd picked up a leather-bound menu.

"Before we discuss Pantara."

"We don't have to do it over breakfast and bore everyone."

But she wasn't going to let herself off the hook. "You need to know I've received an offer to join a new firm, Nester and Hedley in D.C."

Caleb lowered the menu, and looked over at her with those piercing, blue eyes. "Is it a good offer?"

"Yes," she admitted. "It's a very good offer. They're the top, international law firm in the country. It would open up a lot of doors for me, give me a chance to work on issues of enormous significance."

He set the menu down and gave her his full focus. "Are you going to take it?"

"I don't know," she answered honestly.

"When will you know?"

"I told them a week."

"So you might stay with Milburn and Associates?" he pressed.

She struggled not to glance at Travis. "I might stay."

"Can I ask you one more question?"

"Sure."

"Are you looking to find a way to leave Chicago, or did this come at you out of the blue."

"Out of the blue," said Danielle. "That's part of the problem. I like Chicago. I like my clients. And, don't take this as me buttering you up, I like working with Active Equipment. You're a big part of the pull for me to stay put."

Again, she fought not to look at Travis. It had nothing to do with him, she assured herself. Even if she was the kind of person to make a decision based on a man, Vegas with Travis had been just that, Vegas with Travis. It wasn't about to translate into the real world.

"Then let's talk Pantara anyway. You can hitch a ride on the jet today and give us some extra time."

"Are you sure?" It was going to be a very complex project. If she left in a few weeks, her work could all turn out to be a waste of time.

"'Morning, all" Katrina called as she and Reed approached the table. She hopped into the chair next to Danielle, and Reed sat next to her. "What did we miss?"

"Danielle's going to catch a ride home with us this afternoon," said Caleb.

"We're not going home this afternoon," said Katrina. "And neither is Danielle."

Caleb lifted a questioning glance to Reed.

"We're going dancing," Katrina piped in. "You should have told him," she said to Danielle. "We bought great new dresses yesterday, and we have to give them a test run."

Reed gave his brother a helpless shrug. "I'm not about to tell my wife she can't dance."

Danielle jumped in. "If Caleb needs me to—"

"Never mind." Caleb waved off her protest with exaggerated resignation.

"But—"

"We'll catch a commercial flight tomorrow," said Reed.

"I can't stay and dance." Danielle turned to Katrina. "I'm really sorry. I'd love to stay, but I've missed too much work already." If she wasn't careful, Nester and Hedley would be her only option, because Milburn and Associates would be letting her go for nonperformance.

"You can stay if it's billable hours," said Caleb.

Danielle turned sharply. "Oh, no you don't." She wasn't about to let Caleb pay her to stay an extra day in Vegas.

But he ignored her, extracting his cell phone from his shirt pocket. "Danielle, I seriously need to talk to you about Pantara. This is business." He pressed a button and lifted the phone to his ear.

"That's a ridiculous stretch," said Danielle.

Caleb simply waved her off.

"Hey, sweetheart," he said into the phone. Then he paused. "It was terrific. Listen, do you want to go dancing tonight?

He smiled as he listened to whatever Mandy was saying at the other end of the line. "With your sister and my brother, who else? And Danielle's coming, too." Another pause. "No, here. You can come to Vegas."

His grin widened. "Absolutely. Yeah. I'll talk to you in a few hours." He hung up.

"I'll stick around," Travis offered.

Both Caleb and Reed looked over at him in surprise.

He shrugged. "I'm the only single guy you've got, and somebody has to dance with Danielle."

Both Caleb and Reed nodded, seeming to agree that it made perfect sense.

Travis's deep blue eyes shifted to Danielle's, and she felt a wash of decadent longing radiate from her core.

"Hey, Zach." Caleb's sudden call across the restaurant startled her.

Katrina nudged her arm. "What?"

Danielle turned to Katrina in confusion. "Huh?"

"Is something wrong?" Katrina whispered. "You've got a funny look on your face."

"Everything's fine." It was better than fine. Which was very bad. Danielle shouldn't be this happy about spending an extra evening with Travis.

"What's up?" asked Zach as he made his way closer to the table.

"The five of us are staying here 'till tomorrow," said Caleb. "Can you let the pilot know to bring Mandy back? She'll be at the airport in Lyndon."

"Sure thing," said Zach, taking the chair between Reed and Travis.

Travis sat back, looking smug and eminently satisfied.

"What's that?" Katrina asked Travis.

"What's what?" He gazed levelly at his sister.

"You look...I don't know." She turned to Reed. "Did I miss something? Did you guys have strippers last night?"

"Of course not," said Reed.

"We did not," Zach confirmed.

"Then why does Travis look so happy?"

"I'm not happy," said Travis.

But it was obviously a lie. Danielle could only hope she wasn't giving off the same kind of glow. And, if she was, that nobody put two and two together.

* * *

Travis and Caleb had stayed back to pay the limo driver, allowing Reed, Katrina, Danielle and Mandy to go on ahead along the Strip. Katrina was on Reed's arm, wearing something white and silky, with a little bit of purple. She looked fresh and young as she always did. Mandy, who had just arrived on the Active Equipment jet, was in basic black. It was tough to get his middle sister out of her blue jeans and into a dress at all. She rarely wore anything very fancy.

And then there was Danielle. Her dress was strapless, tight, gold and sparkling across her body, then fanning into a short, stiff, multi-layered skirt, scattered with gold sequins that winked under the lights. Her legs were long and shapely, ending in strappy gold sandals. She outshone every woman on the block.

"My brother's attracting a lot of attention," Caleb joked.

It was true. As people passed Reed and the three women, they craned their necks, clearly wondering who he was to warrant three gorgeous dates.

"At least he makes a good bodyguard," said Travis, thinking he'd better not let Danielle wander around alone tonight. He'd have to stick close to her side to keep the wolves at bay. Which he was totally willing, no, make that eager, to do.

"Hey," Caleb interrupted his thoughts, an accusation in his tone.

"What?" Travis glanced around, trying to figure out what was wrong.

"I can see the way you're lookin' at my lawyer."

"It's the same way every other guy is looking at your lawyer," Travis quickly retorted.

"They're not dancing with her."

"Too bad for them."

"I'm serious, Travis. You can't be messin' with Danielle. She's too important to Active Equipment for you to make her mad."

"I'm fifteen feet away from her."

"Promise me you won't try anything."

"Don't be ridiculous," Travis scoffed.

"I'm not being ridiculous. I want your word on that."

Travis shot Caleb an exasperated look. "Why are you being so paranoid?"

"Because you're not promising me anything."

"We aren't ten-year-old girls. I'm not going to pinky swear."

"Travis," Caleb intoned. "Why are you being deliberately vague about this?"

"Because it's none of your business."

"It is my business, exactly. How is it not my business?"

"We're consenting adults."

"You're not—" Caleb stopped short, voice going low. "*What* did you do?"

"I'm not going to answer that. Besides, Danielle getting ticked off at me is not your biggest risk. Your biggest risk is her dream job in D.C."

It was clear that answer got Caleb thinking.

Travis took advantage. "If I was you, I'd be convincing her that the Pantara project is worth her giving up D.C."

"The Pantara project *is* worth her giving up D.C."

"You've got nearly a week to play with." Travis felt guilty about what he was doing here, but not guilty enough to stop. "Bring her back to Lyndon Valley for a few days and convince her."

Caleb focused on Travis again, sizing him up. "You want me to bring Danielle back to Lyndon Valley?"

"You know Nester and Hedley will be working on her. You know Randal will be trying to convince her to take the D.C. job. Hell, he might even head for Chicago and track her down in person."

"Who's Randal?"

"A guy from Nester and Hedley."

"Just a guy?" Caleb probed.

"Just a guy."

They started walking again.

"And you'll be okay with that?" asked Caleb. "With Danielle spending a few days in Lyndon Valley."

Travis shrugged, trying to look unconcerned, as if he couldn't care less one way or the other. "Sure."

Throbbing music rose in volume as they neared the Aster Club's entrance. Voices also rose from the long line of patrons and carried across the sidewalk.

If Danielle was in Lyndon Valley, he reasoned, she was away from Randal. She was also with Travis. Not that he expected her to give him the time of day back home. She'd been pretty clear that this was a Vegas thing only. Still, better she was with him than somewhere she might fall into Randal's clutches.

Caleb's tone turned even more serious. "What's going on, Travis?"

"Why does something have to be going on? Danielle's been to Lyndon Valley lots of times before."

"And you always fight with her there. And now you're dancing with her?"

"Take a look at that." Travis nodded to where Reed had walked boldly up to the VIP entrance.

The bouncer unclipped the velvet rope and gestured them forward.

"I guess three gorgeous women will do that for you," said Caleb quickly picking up the pace to catch up.

Travis did the same.

The bouncer put the flat of his hand on Caleb's chest.

"We're with them," Caleb explained. "Mandy, honey?" he called.

Mandy turned. "That's my husband," she called back to the bouncer, but the man seemed unimpressed.

"I won Bull Mania Saturday night," Travis offered.

The man's eyes narrowed, then his expression changed to a welcoming smile. "I recognize you. Come on in."

Caleb gaped at him. "You have got to be kidding."

"Works ever better if I bring along the belt buckle."

"That's sad."

"You think that's sad. Let me tell you about my complimentary hotel suite."

Caleb gave a baffled shake of his head as they made their way through the entry hall.

Inside the Aster Club, Travis beelined for Danielle. He could already see the interested looks from other men, and he wasn't leaving her alone for a second.

He wrapped an arm around her waist. "You want to dance first or drink first?"

Her lips curved into a dazzling smile. "Dance."

"Okay." He led her through the crowds and into the bright colored light.

He didn't see where Caleb or Reed had gone, and he didn't particularly care. He twirled Danielle, laughing, into his arms. The music was loud and vibrant. There was no point in trying to talk, so they simply danced.

She was light in his arms, sensitive to his lead. She was fun to dance with, but as they moved through the songs, their spins and dips decreased, while their holds became longer and more frequent. On the fourth song, the DJ slowed things down, and Travis pulled her close, settling her against his chest.

He inhaled the fresh fragrance of her hair, felt her curves nestle into him, and tipped his head toward her bare shoulders. If Caleb caught sight of him and Danielle, there wouldn't be a doubt left in his mind what was going on. But Travis didn't care. His time with Danielle was going to be limited one way or the other, and he was going to make the most of what he had.

As the song wound down, she tilted her head back. It was hard for him to resist kissing her.

"I'm getting thirsty," she told him.

"This way, then." He linked her arm in his, maneuvering their way off the crowded dance floor.

They cleared the light show, traversed the length of the bar, finding a quieter corner with soft furniture, low tables and muted lighting. They chose a section of a curved, bench sofa in an empty grouping, each sitting on one side of a curve, knees close together.

A white shirted waiter immediately arrived. "Can I get you a drink?"

"Mojito for me," said Danielle.

"I'll take the same," said Travis.

Danielle raised her brows. "You're sure you want to trust my taste in drinks?"

"I figure you've got to get it right sometime."

She looked to the waiter. "Bring him a beer. Anything from DFB."

The waiter glanced to him for confirmation.

"Aren't you bossy."

"I am." She sat back on the sofa.

"I'll take the beer," Travis confirmed. "I like your dress," he told Danielle as the waiter walked away.

Sitting down, she looked even better if that was possible. The dress accentuated her perfect breasts, showed off the indent of her slender waist, empha-sized her creamy, smooth shoulders and her grace-ful neck. And those legs. If he could have designed a perfect pair of legs, they would be Danielle's.

"Thanks," she smiled, picking up the mini menu in the center of the table. "You hungry?"

"I'd eat. What do you feel like?"

"Something spicy." She let the menu fall open in her hands.

"There you are," came Katrina's breathy voice.

Travis's sister plunked down into one of the rounded chairs across the table from Danielle. Reed took one look at the size of its mate, and moved to the end of the sofa instead.

"Any interest in a Thai platter?" asked Danielle.

"I'd go for that," said Katrina. "And Reed'll eat anything."

"This is true," Reed agreed easily. "Living in New York, I've discovered I have an international palette."

"That's a very gracious way of putting it," said Travis.

The waiter arrived, and Katrina immediately pointed to the mojito. "I'll take one of those."

"Is that DFB?" Reed asked, pointing to Travis's beer.

"C Mountain Ale," said Travis as he accepted it.

"Sounds good to me," said Reed.

"We'd like the Thai platter," Travis told the waiter. "And bring us some of the barbecue sliders as well."

Danielle nudged his knee. "You can take the cowboy off the range?" she asked him, tone lightly teasing.

"I guess I'm not as international as Reed." Their gazes met and locked, and it took him a moment to break it.

"Hey, all." It was Mandy's voice this time. She was followed by Caleb who stopped the waiter to place their drink order.

Mandy took the chair next to Katrina, and Caleb took the one around the end of the table from her.

"At least Alex and Zach made it home from the bachelor party," said Mandy.

"They've got the most to do," said Reed.

Alex was marrying the Jacobses' cousin Lisa, while their brother-in-law Zach was his best man. Zach and Alex had started DFB brewery together years ago, only recently moving it to Lyndon Valley.

"The rest of you will have to come home eventually," said Mandy.

"Tomorrow, for sure," said Caleb. Then he glanced at Katrina. "Right?"

"Sadly, yes," she agreed. "But Danielle and I had to have a chance to show off our dresses."

Mandy glanced to Danielle. "I can sure tell Katrina helped you pick that out."

Danielle frowned as she glanced down. "It's not exactly my usual style, is it?"

Travis couldn't help jumping in. "Just because she's a lawyer, doesn't mean she's staid."

He received surprised looks from his sisters.

"Who said she was staid?" asked Katrina.

"We love Danielle," Mandy put in staunchly. "You should stop picking on her, Travis."

Caleb coughed in obvious amusement.

"What is wrong with you?" Mandy asked her husband. "Do you have a problem with Danielle's sense of style?"

"Of course not," said Caleb. "I trust Danielle's sense of everything. I'm hoping to send her to Europe."

Mandy's tone changed to one of eagerness. "We're going to Europe?"

"Danielle's going to Europe. Why? You want to go, too?"

Mandy gave an eager nod. "Maybe for a few days?"

Travis felt Danielle shift beside him. He could guess what she was thinking. If she took the job in

D.C., she wouldn't be going anywhere for Active Equipment. He silently thanked his brother-in-law for making her choice perhaps a little more complicated.

"Have you made a decision about D.C. yet?" Travis asked Danielle.

It was nine in the morning, and he was shaving at one of the bathroom sinks in his suite while she applied a layer of mascara at its twin.

"I have five days left," she reminded him, holding her eyes wide for a moment so that her makeup wouldn't smear.

They were hurrying to meet the others in the lobby for the trip to the airport. She'd picked up her suitcase on the way to his suite last night. When they got back from the club, there'd seemed no point in her being coy about wanting to spend their final night together.

"You must be leaning one way or the other." He used a towel to wipe the excess shaving cream from his neck.

"I'm leaning toward putting the decision off as long as possible." She wanted to do both. It was impossible, of course, but that was what she wanted.

Travis turned to look at her profile. "You know he's going to lobby you to come to D.C."

She gazed at his reflection in the mirror as she applied some lip gloss. "Are you lobbying me on Caleb's behalf?"

"I'm not on my brother-in-law's payroll."

"Then, why are you asking?"

"Because Randal will lobby you," Travis told her with conviction. "And he's got his own agenda."

"Is this an I-told-you-so lecture? Because I already conceded to you on that point."

"This is a 'his agenda is not in your best interest' lecture."

She tucked her lip gloss and mascara back in her makeup bag, running a comb through her now dry hair. She really didn't want to have this conversation with Travis. He might be a macho, overprotective cowboy, but her life was hers, and she could take very good care of herself.

"I'm a big girl, Travis. And I'm reasonably intelligent."

He looked surprised, his face reflecting in the mirror. "I didn't mean to insult you."

She found herself growing impatient. "You're not insulting me. You're crowding me." She pivoted to face him. "I just spent the last two days in *your* bed, not in his."

"And I bet he knows it."

"So what?"

"So, it'll make him want you even more."

"Really? Truly? That's what you want to say to me this morning? That by sleeping with me, you've somehow made Randal more attracted to me? As if I couldn't do that all on my own."

"Whoa." Travis drew back.

"No, you whoa, cowboy." She lifted her makeup bag, deciding to make a swift exit. "You're a fun guy, and a good lover, but we're about to go back to our real lives, so you can stop fretting about what I'm going to do next."

He went silent for a beat. "Caleb will be upset if you leave."

She shook her head, forcing down the reflexive guilt she felt for even thinking about taking the D.C. job. "No, Travis. You don't get to use Caleb or Reed or Katrina against me. This is my life, and one weekend with me does not give you the right to interfere."

"I'm not interfering."

She headed for the bathroom door. "This is my decision."

He followed, and they emerged into the airy, opulent bedroom. "Of course it's your decision. I never said it wasn't."

Her suitcase was sitting on the mussed up bed,

and she tossed in the makeup case and zipped it shut. "You're as bad as Randal."

"I'm nothing like Randal."

"Then let me figure this out on my own."

"I am."

"Good." She stepped into her shoes, glancing at her watch. "We're out of time."

"Yeah." His voice sounded hollow. He stared at her a moment longer then lifted the suitcase from the bed, moving toward the living room.

She slung her purse over her shoulder and followed him out.

"You want to go down first?" he asked her.

"Sure."

She met his eyes. She didn't want to fight. But she felt the need to protect herself from him encroaching on her life after they left Vegas. The interlude had been exciting, mind-blowing, completely unforgettable. But it had to end, and it had to end right here.

"I don't know what to say," he admitted.

"I think you want to say goodbye."

A muscle flexed near his right eye, but he didn't answer.

"Goodbye, Travis," she offered.

"Don't you dare try to shake my hand."

Before she could react, he drew her tight into his arms.

"Goodbye, Danielle," he whispered against her ear. "You call me if you—"

"Don't," she interrupted, pulling back.

"—ever need anything," he finished.

"I'm not going to need anything," she denied. She'd gotten along perfectly well, some might say extraordinarily well, in her life before he came along.

He gave a nod of acceptance. "Good luck with your decision. Somebody's going to be incredibly lucky to get you."

For some reason the compliment made her uncomfortable. She tried to make light of it. "Only until I make my first big mistake."

"You don't make mistakes, Danielle."

"Oh, yes I do. And I will. And when I do, well…"

She stopped. She realized she was rattling on, postponing that moment when she'd have to walk out his door.

"I have to go." She gave him a fleeting kiss on the mouth, then broke eye contact and extended the handle of her suitcase, tipping it onto its wheels.

Travis hesitated, but then he moved to open the suite door.

"I'll see you down there."

"Thanks," she nodded without looking at him and forced herself to walk through the door.

Shoulders squared, head held high, she quickly moved along the length of the hallway to the elevators. She didn't hear Travis close the door behind her, but she didn't look back. She rounded the corner, pressed the call button, and told herself to buck up.

Her future was square in front of her. Randal's unwelcome attention notwithstanding, D.C. was an excellent move for her to make. Caleb could find another lawyer. There were hundreds of other good lawyers in Chicago. Six months from now, Active Equipment wouldn't even miss her. Heck, they probably wouldn't miss her six weeks from now. She'd make sure her replacement was totally up to speed.

The elevator door opened silently in front of her.

Somebody else could manage the merger. Somebody else could go to Europe. And she'd never see Travis again.

The elevator started downward, it left her stomach behind.

# Eight

On the plane ride back to Lyndon Valley, Caleb had asked Danielle to stay and work with him on the Pantara merger from their ranch for a few days. It seemed Mandy's favorite mare had fallen sick, and she didn't want to leave Lyndon Valley right away.

Danielle understood Caleb's desire to be near his wife, but she was anxious to get back to Chicago. Beyond the emotional complication of being so near to Travis, she needed to spend some time in her own office. She wanted to ponder what she'd be giving up by moving to D.C., maybe clean up her files, put herself in a position to make the move— if she decided she wanted to make the move.

But Caleb was her client, so she'd agreed to stay. She put her energy toward making contacts in Germany and working with international stock exchange listings. She struggled hard not to think about Travis being just down the road, tried not to wonder what he was doing, alternately hoping he would call and then being glad he hadn't. She'd been at the Terrell Ranch for a day and a half, and she hadn't had any contact at all with him. Not that she was paying attention. Talking to him would truly be a bad idea. Seeing him would be even worse.

Footsteps sounded in the hall, and Caleb appeared in the entry of the small office on the second floor of the ranch house.

"It's nearly six," he informed her.

"That's two in the morning in Germany. They'll be back at the office in six hours." She was polishing a memo to have in Pantara's inbox when they arrived in the morning.

"All the more reason for you to stop working."

Danielle clicked open the attachment on an email. "I've got some German case law I wanted to go over on foreign ownership in strategic industry sectors."

Caleb moved into the room. "Anyone ever tell you you're a workaholic."

She glanced up at him, blinking in mock astonishment. "I'm sorry. *You're* accusing *me* of being a workaholic?"

"I'm a business owner," said Caleb. "I'm supposed to work 24/7."

"I'm billing you for all these hours," she informed him, scanning the index page of the document she'd just opened.

"I'm responsible for keeping you from working yourself to death."

"It's barely six o'clock, Caleb." When she was in Chicago, she rarely left the office before seven. And here, she didn't need to commute through traffic. She scrolled down to the executive summary of the paper.

"What time are you getting up?" he asked.

She hadn't decided yet, but likely around four. It was always a challenge to operate across overseas time zones.

"Mandy's putting burgers on the grill."

"Could she save one for me?"

"Travis is here."

Danielle's attention shot to Caleb. She swallowed, struggling to keep her expression neutral.

"I invited him up for a burger."

"That's nice."

It was obviously going to happen eventually. The Terrells and Jacobses were lifelong friends. She knew from spending time on the ranch in the past that they dropped into each other's places all the time. Travis was Mandy's brother. Of course he'd want to spend time with her while she was in Lyndon Valley.

Caleb cocked his head toward the door. "Let's go."

She glanced back at the computer screen. "I wanted to go through—"

"You have to eat."

She supposed that was true. But if she scanned the executive summary right now, she could come back later and zero in on the salient points. Plus, it would give her a few minutes to prepare herself for seeing Travis again.

"I'll be right down," she told Caleb.

"You're coming with me now."

"You don't trust me?"

"I trust you to get your nose buried in that paper and forget all about eating, sleeping and everything else."

Danielle knew she wasn't about to forget about Travis. He was downstairs, merely one floor below her. How should she act? What should she say?

"Danielle?"

"I'm coming," she capitulated, hitting the save button.

She'd treat him as a friend—no, as an acquaintance. She wouldn't fight with him, like she usually did. But she wouldn't say or do anything to allude to their fling, either. She'd be polite but distant, professional.

She rose from the desk chair and followed Caleb out of the office. They made their way to the end of the hall and down the staircase to the farmhouse living room. Voices came through the kitchen, the smell of barbecue smoke on the evening air. Mandy and Travis were obviously on the deck.

"Wine?" asked Caleb as they rounded the corner.

"Absolutely," she answered, just as she caught sight of Travis.

She stopped dead at the sight. He was laughing with Mandy, stance relaxed and easy, a bottle of beer in one hand. Dressed in a faded denim shirt and a worn pair of jeans, he looked completely at home against the backdrop of the mountains and the Lyndon River below. Her heart did a triple beat inside her chest.

"It's a merlot," said Caleb.

"Huh?" She gave herself a mental shake.

Caleb held up a bottle of red. "Merlot."

"Sounds great," she managed.

He snagged a wine glass from a shelf.

Mandy caught sight of her.

"Hey, Danielle," she called, grinning as she waved the spatula.

Travis swiveled his head, and their eyes met. A wave of energy passed through the air between them. Danielle felt it from the roots of her hair to the tips of her toes.

"Here you go," said Caleb, holding out the glass of wine.

"Thanks." She accepted the glass and took a big swallow.

"Thirsty?" asked Caleb.

"Very." She forcibly dragged her gaze from Travis.

Caleb turned to round the kitchen's island and head out the double doors.

Danielle forced herself to follow, telling herself to be professional. She could do this.

"Hello, Travis," she offered brightly. "Nice to see you again."

There was a brief moment of confusion in his eyes. "Hello, Danielle."

"How are things at the ranch?" she asked, choosing a deck chair near the rail to get herself off her wobbly legs.

"Same old, same old," he answered, pulling a chair from the dining table to face her. "Cattle, horses, broken water pumps."

"Were you able to fix it?" she asked.

"Ask him about the accounting software," Mandy suggested.

"The water pump was no problem," Travis answered.

"With Amanda gone, we tried to streamline the books," Mandy put in. "The new computer system is going to be the death of him."

Travis turned to peer at his sister. "I didn't sign up to do paperwork."

"Dail-E Entries?" asked Danielle.

"That's the one," answered Mandy.

"How did you know?" asked Travis.

"It's the most popular. If you take the tutorial, it's pretty straightforward."

"Travis, follow the instructions?" Mandy mocked.

Caleb laughed.

Travis frowned. "I don't have time to learn from a cartoon dog that talks to me like I'm a five-year-old. I've got real work to do."

"So, you tried the tutorial?" Danielle asked, struggling not to be amused by his obvious frustration.

"I made it through lesson three. Then I went outside and branded some steers instead."

Danielle grinned, feeling more relaxed. She sipped at the tasty merlot.

"You should go down give him a hand," Mandy

said to Danielle. "You could probably show him how to work the system in a fraction of the time it would take to do the tutorials."

So much for relaxed. The last thing she needed was to be alone with Travis. "I'm pretty busy with Pantara."

"I can spare you for a few hours," Caleb offered easily.

Danielle looked to Travis, meeting his deep blue eyes. The energy vortex was pulling her in again.

"It'd be a big help," he said, expression perfectly neutral.

She had no idea whether he wanted to get her alone, or whether he truly wanted help with his accounting software. Either way, she'd look churlish if she refused.

"Sure," she offered, slugging back the last of her wine, kicking herself for having opened her mouth in the first place. "I can give him a hand."

Travis wanted to get this right. He didn't want to overstep, but he didn't want to pretend nothing had happened in Vegas either. Last night, Danielle had been polite but distant. Sure, Mandy and Caleb had been there the whole time, but she hadn't let on for a second that there'd ever been anything between them.

This morning, she was coming down to the Jacobses' ranch. He'd worked for a few hours, then he'd stopped to shower and shave, not wanting to offend her while they were working in close quarters. The ranch office was tiny, little more than a converted storage closet off the living room. It had a small desk and chair, a file cabinet and a computer. Travis had pulled in a stool for himself, so they'd both be able to sit down.

There was a knock on the front door. His chest tightened, knowing it had to be Danielle. Nobody else would bother with that formality.

He popped a mint in his mouth, reflexively straightened his shirt, glanced around the cluttered room, then headed across the living room to the entry foyer. Jackets, boots, hats and gloves littered a row of hooks and a bank of cubbyholes. He'd never given a moment's thought to the mess, but now he wondered what the utilitarian house looked like to Danielle.

She probably lived in a sleek, modern apartment. Maybe she had white, leather furniture and chrome fixtures. She probably had a cleaning lady who dusted her fine art and kept exotic plants looking lush and green. The only things Travis grew were oats and sweet grass.

He swung open the door.

"I'm only here to help with the software," she announced, expression stern, her eyes dark and serious.

She wore a pair of designer jeans, brown fashion boots and a dark blazer over a silver blouse. Her short hair had lifted in the breeze, but ended up chic rather than messy. She carried a big shoulder purse that was saddle bag brown. Somehow, she managed to look both city and country at the same time.

"Software is my current problem," he responded, stepping to one side and gesturing her in.

Not that he didn't plan to have other problems in the future—chief among them, an overpowering urge to pull her back into his arms. For now, he wished he could to erase this formality between them, get back to the intimacy they'd shared in Vegas. Those nights they were in his hotel suite, he'd felt closer to her than he'd ever been with a woman.

She stepped over the threshold. "Point me to your office."

He did. "Through that door."

She gave a nod and started walking.

"Can I get you anything?" he called to her back. "Coffee? Juice?"

She didn't bother turning as she answered. "Coffee would be good. Does your computer have a password?"

*"Wrangler."*

That time, she turned. "Seriously?"

He shrugged. "It seemed appropriate, easy for everyone to remember."

"We should talk security sometime."

"Sure. What do you want in your coffee?"

"Black," she responded.

He couldn't help but grin.

"What?"

"I was just trying to decide if you were more city or country. Black coffee is a good start."

Her gaze narrowed. "Is black coffee city or country?"

"Country, ma'am."

"I don't know about that."

"If you'd asked for a caramel, chocolate mocha with whipped cream, I'd have gone the other way."

"Aren't you the biased, judgmental cowboy?"

He just grinned, turning for the kitchen. "Log-on name is *Jacobs,*" he called over his shoulder.

"Of course it is. You probably also have a welcome mat for hackers."

There was a pot of hot coffee in the kitchen, so Travis was quickly back in the office with a stoneware mug in each hand. Danielle had taken the chair, and he set the blue mug down on the desk beside her. Then he perched himself on the stool over her left shoulder.

"This is the main menu." She pointed with her mouse.

"I got that much," he responded, taking a sip of the hot brew.

"On a daily basis, you'll need the top three items, entering payable, entering receivables, and printing checks. These next three are reports, including a balance sheet. And the rest are for setting up master files, doing audits and occasional trouble shooting."

She turned to look up at him. "So far, so good?"

"I understand the main menu," he responded, thinking she was beautiful. She smelled amazing. He could only hope he'd be able to drag his attention from her long enough to learn the other elements of the software.

"Glad to hear it." She turned back.

"Double click on payables, and it opens up a date entry screen." She demonstrated as she spoke.

The screen that came up in front of them showed about twenty fields, everything from vendor name to shipping date.

"Do you have a vendor master file set up?"

"No."

"Seriously?" She closed the screen.

"Sorry," he felt compelled to offer.

She heaved a sigh. "This is going to take longer than I thought."

As far as Travis was concerned, that was good news. He liked having her here. The longer it took, the better his chances of—

He stopped himself. His chances of what? He didn't want to seduce her. Not that he wouldn't give his eye teeth to sleep with her again, but that wasn't why he wanted her to stay.

He just wanted to be with her, he realized. Hear her voice, talk with her, joke with her, argue with her, find out what she was thinking about the D.C. job and about a hundred other things.

"Travis?" Her tone was sharp, and she smacked him on the knee.

He realized she'd been talking just then, and he hadn't heard a word. "What?"

"I said I'm going to show you how to create a vendor master file. You build it tonight, and I'll come back in the morning."

Oh, that didn't sound good. "How does that work?" he asked, mind searching for a way to make her stay. Ten minutes in her company simply wasn't going to do it for him. He'd been looking forward to seeing her all night long.

"Here." She clicked the mouse through a couple

of menus. "You need to enter all of your supplier's tombstone information, and the system will assign them a five-digit number. That's your vendor ID."

"I type with two fingers," he lied. "There's no way I can enter all that stuff tonight."

She closed her eyes for a long moment. "You have got to be kidding me."

"No, ma'am."

"You do realize I have a whole other job."

"Yes, I do." But he couldn't seem to bring himself to care about that at the moment.

"And you do realize your brother-in-law is paying several hundred dollars an hour for me to type for you?"

"He offered," Travis defended, silently thanking Caleb for setting this whole thing up.

"So, I have to type in all of your vendors before we can even start."

Travis gave a shrug of innocence.

"Do you at least have a list of their names and contact information?"

"Maybe." He stood up and maneuvered his way to the cabinet. "I know they each have their own file folder."

"Give me strength," Danielle breathed from behind him.

Travis opened the drawer, pulling the first file. "Should I read them out to you?"

"If that's the best we can do, that's the best we can do."

"Acme Feed and Supply," he began. "Seventeen twenty-two, Rosedale Road."

Danielle's fingers clicked on the computer keys while Travis worked his way through the files.

At Streamline Irrigation Equipment, she finally agreed to break for lunch.

They left the office and worked together in the kitchen, making stacked sandwiches on rye bread, with turkey, cheese, tomatoes and cucumbers. Travis retrieved a pitcher of iced tea from the fridge, and they perched on stools around the island breakfast bar.

"This is a big job for one person, isn't it?" she opened before biting down on her sandwich.

"Running the ranch?" he asked, surprised that her mind might have gone to that.

She nodded.

"It is," he agreed.

He knew he'd have to find himself some additional help of some kind. But he hadn't quite wrapped his head around what that might be. The place had gone from a family of six, excluding

Katrina, with a wide variety of skill sets, down to only him in less than two years.

"Do you think Seth might come back and help you?"

"Not anytime soon. The railway project is going to take at least a couple of years."

"Maybe you should find yourself a wife," she suggested.

He frowned as he bit into his own sandwich. If he had a wife, he couldn't sleep with Danielle anymore.

"Someone who can rope and ride and cook and type," she continued. "I'm sure there are plenty of nice ranch girls in Colorado who know their way around a personal computer."

"Maybe I can take out an ad and collect resumes," he offered dryly.

"You could fill out an online dating profile. Just be specific about what you want."

"Is that how you're planning to do it?"

She sucked something from the tip of her thumb. "I don't need a man."

"Right, I forgot. Self-sufficiency is your mantra."

He didn't know why he was getting annoyed, but he was. He should be happy that she wasn't interested in a serious relationship. That should leave Randal out in the cold.

"It is," she agreed. "And I don't have a ranch to run. My condo is pretty low maintenance. No livestock or irrigation equipment." She grinned into her sandwich. "Good thing. It's probably against the zoning bylaws anyway."

"What makes you so cheerful?" he couldn't help asking.

A few minutes ago, she'd been clearly frustrated at having to spend so much time helping him. Now, talking about marrying him off, all of a sudden she was bubbly and joking.

"You're complaining because I'm too happy?"

"I don't know why you want to see me married in such a hurry."

"I was only suggesting it as a means to divide the workload."

"Yeah, well if I marry some Colorado ranch girl, I'm going to have to sleep with her."

"That's the generally accepted convention. Though, legally speaking, it doesn't necessarily nullify the marriage if you don't."

He couldn't seem to help the annoyance churning its way through his stomach. "Legally speaking?"

"Yes."

Their gazes met and held.

"I'm guessing she'll expect it," he noted.

"I'm guessing she will."

"And if I don't want to?" he asked softly.

"Then, you'll probably have some explaining to do."

The room went silent between them. The only woman he wanted to sleep with was Danielle. Did she know that? Could she guess that?

"I've missed you," he told her.

"Don't."

He reached for her hand, taking it in his own. "You want me to pretend I didn't miss you?" He was tired of tiptoeing around his feelings, of measuring his every word.

She looked him straight in the eyes. "Yes."

For some reason, her answer amused him. "Do you also want me to pretend I'm not attracted to you?"

"That would be helpful."

"Why?"

"All the regular reasons."

"There are regular reasons? What are the regular reasons?"

She thought about it for a moment. "For starters, because I'm me, and you're you." She stretched her arm around the kitchen. "You have to take care of all this. Which is good, which is great. But I'm only going to be here for a couple more days. After that…" She paused. "After that, I have to…" She pulled her hand from his.

Travis's chest tightened. "You're going to take it aren't you."

At first she didn't answer.

A cold feeling of dread moved through his stomach. "Danielle?"

"Yes," she whispered. "I'm going to take it. I have to take it." Her voice grew stronger. "It's a once-in-a-lifetime opportunity to do exactly what I want to do with my career."

"And Randal?"

Her eyes narrowed. "What about Randal?"

"He's going to be there."

Her tone went tight. "And?"

Travis couldn't seem to stop himself. "And, you know he wants you. He's not going to give up."

The thought of Randal seeing her every day, having an open field to charm her and convince her. It might take him weeks or months, but eventually, he might succeed. They'd been an item once before.

"I can handle Randal," said Danielle.

"Can you?" Travis demanded. "Can you really?

Her face flushed. "What kind of a question is that?"

"You didn't do so well *handling him* in Vegas.

You didn't see it coming. You wouldn't even believe me until it was almost too late."

"Almost too late for *what*?"

"He tried to kiss you."

She came to her feet. "And I stopped him."

"Do you think that settles it?"

"It settles it in my mind."

"Not in his. He's regrouping, re-strategizing. He's going to come at you all over again with a new game plan." Travis couldn't let this happen. With every fiber of his being, he knew he couldn't let this happen.

Her eyes went dark with anger, and her jaw clenched down tight. "That's got nothing to do with you."

He knew that was true, but he didn't care. "You can't go to D.C."

She was silent for a long while. Then she shook her head. "Watch me." She turned on her heel and walked out.

Danielle's heart was pounding and her hands were still shaking as she brought the car to a halt in front of the Terrell ranch house. Travis's questions had made her angry. His demands had infuriated her. Her career was none of his business.

Randal was none of his business. None of this was any of his business.

She rammed the gearshift into Park and turned the key.

The idea that she couldn't manage Randal was ridiculous. It was insulting. Yes, sure, Travis had seen it coming before she had. But Danielle was the one Randal tried to kiss. She was the one who'd held him off. She'd told him no. She'd set down the ground rules. She was absolutely and completely capable of taking care of herself in D.C.

She exited the car, slamming the door harder than necessary. Then she stalked her way to the porch.

She'd slept with Travis twice. Big deal. They'd promised to leave it in Vegas. Well, she'd left it all in Vegas. As far as she was concerned, he was Caleb's neighbor, Katrina's brother, nothing more, nothing less.

She entered the ranch house, closing the door firmly behind her.

Okay, so maybe she still had the hots for him. Maybe she missed him. Maybe she couldn't stop dreaming about him. Again, big deal. Nobody got everything they wanted in life.

"Danielle?" came Katrina's voice.

"I'm back," Danielle called out, struggling to keep the anger out of her voice.

"What's wrong?" Katrina appeared in the entry hall. "You sound upset. You look—" Katrina peered at her. "What the heck?"

Danielle knew she couldn't brush it off completely. "I had a fight with Travis," she confessed, bracing herself for the worst.

"Is that all?" asked Katrina, expression neutralizing. "You fight with him all the time."

"Yes," Danielle agreed. "I do." A little bit of the tension left her stomach.

Maybe this was a good thing. Fighting with Travis was certainly more normal than sleeping with him. Although, their fights hadn't used to upset her this much. Then again, their fights had never been this personal before. Maybe she could look at this as a step back to their old relationship. It was worth a try.

"Did you get the software up and running?" asked Katrina.

"Partway," Danielle answered. "We ran out of time," she lied.

"I think Caleb will be glad to have you back." Katrina moved toward the living room, and Danielle went with her.

"Is something wrong?"

Katrina glanced at the stairs. "Judging by the language I'm hearing. Yes."

"Uh-oh." Danielle headed for the staircase.

"So, you'll finish tomorrow?" called Katrina.

"Pantara?" Were they done? Could she go back to Chicago now? That would be great news. She'd love to put Lyndon Valley in her rearview mirror.

Katrina looked at her as if she'd lost her mind. "The accounting software. Will you finish with Travis tomorrow?"

It was on the tip of Danielle's tongue to announce that she'd already finished with Travis. But that would only provoke questions.

"I think he'll be fine on his own now," she answered instead.

"That's great," said Katrina.

A string of swearwords echoed down the stairs.

Danielle glanced up. "Oh, that doesn't sound good."

"I've been afraid to investigate," Katrina confessed.

Danielle couldn't help hoping it was Pantara. Then again, she hoped it was a problem she could solve. She paused, realizing she would have to solve it in only three days.

She was almost out of time. Very soon, she'd have to tell Caleb her decision.

She mounted the stairs.

When she peeped into the office, Caleb had his phone to his ear. He motioned her forward.

"That's not good enough, Stan." Caleb paused. "Tell them no way in hell. Tell them we've got an ironclad contract. There is no loophole. And tell them to source the raw materials out of Brazil if they have to and pay the extra freight."

Danielle could tell he was talking to Stan Buchannan, the president of their South American division.

She sat down to wait for him to finish.

"Yeah," Caleb said gruffly. "Call me after." He hung up the phone.

"Trouble?" she asked, relieved to be back on familiar ground.

"I need you to go through the Greystoke contract. They want to backorder us on steel."

Danielle sat up straight. "They can't do that."

"That's exactly what I said." He gave a sheepish grin. "Well, I said a few other things, too."

"Won't that shut down the Columbia plant?" She moved to the computer desk, typing her log-in and password to the Active Equipment server.

"It sure will," said Caleb.

"It's all in Annex P," she spoke as she typed. "You'll be able to sue them into bankruptcy."

"I don't want to sue anyone. I want my production lines to keep running."

"You think threats will help?"

"I think they need to know exactly the consequences if they mess with me."

"On it, boss."

"That's what I like to hear."

Katrina appeared in the doorway. "Has the storm subsided?"

"For now," said Caleb, coming to his feet. "Sorry you had to hear all that."

"Danielle, I just talked to Travis."

Danielle's fingers faltered on the computer keys.

"He says he does need you to come back tomorrow. Something about finishing the vendor master file and looking at the payables system?"

"He'll be able to figure it out," said Danielle, blindly scrolling her way through the contract.

Katrina hesitated. "I know you were arguing, but maybe you should call him directly. There seems to be some confusion."

"Maybe later," said Danielle. "I need to get through this for Caleb right away."

"Sure," Katrina replied.

There was a moment of silence, before Danielle heard her walk back down the hall.

Thankfully, her vision cleared, and she was able to find Annex P.

"What's the confusion?" asked Caleb, moving up behind her.

Danielle swallowed. "I don't know. He's stubborn."

"No kidding."

"It's all there in the instructions."

Caleb paused. "What was the argument about?"

Danielle was losing her concentration again.

"Same old, same old," she offered airily. "But I really need to focus here."

"I know what happened between you two in Vegas."

Mortification washed through her. She spoke before she could stop herself. "Travis *told* you?"

"I guessed. He didn't deny it. And now, neither are you."

She shook her head at her own foolishness. She should have pretended she didn't know what Caleb was talking about.

"It was nothing," she told him now. "It's nothing. It was nothing, and it's over."

"Okay." Caleb's voice was calm and kind.

In her peripheral vision, she saw him sit down. "So, what was the argument about?"

Danielle knew it was time to tell him the truth. She turned to face him, screwing up her courage.

"I'm sorry."

"You have absolutely nothing to be sorry about. You're an adult, and—"

"Oh, no. Not that." She felt her face heat. "Travis is angry because I told him I was taking the D.C. job." Nervousness gripped her stomach. "I'm sorry about that, Caleb. The opportunity is just too good to turn down."

He smiled understandingly. "It's your decision, Danielle."

"I hate that I'm leaving you," she confessed. "I love working with Active Equipment. And this new project with Pantara. It's going to be huge, Caleb. You know that, don't you?"

He nodded. "I know it's going to be huge. I'd truly love to have you there with me."

For a second, Danielle was afraid she might tear up. She could barely speak. "I'm sorry."

"And I'm sorry Travis upset you. Your decisions are yours alone. He's got to respect that."

"That's what I told him."

"Good for you."

Caleb was such an understanding man, such an incredibly professional business owner, her behavior with Travis in Vegas suddenly seemed worse than ever. She felt like she had to explain.

"Travis and me," she began.

But Caleb shook his head. "Is none of my business."

"But I was there working for you. And he's your brother-in-law. And—"

"Stop talking, Danielle."

She pressed her lips together.

"My advice?" he asked.

She was a little afraid to hear it. "Sure."

"Go back tomorrow and talk to him."

Before Caleb was even finished speaking, she was shaking her head. "You don't understand."

"I understand that you're upset, and that's not good. Knowing Travis, he said something stupid. But he's a hothead, he blows up fast and cools down faster. I'm betting he wants to make it better."

She swallowed convulsively, tears threatening once more. "It's not that simple."

It wasn't just that she was angry with Travis. She was afraid of her own emotions. She didn't want to leave him. In his kitchen this afternoon, she'd come dangerously close to making a career decision based on a man. She couldn't do that, *wouldn't* do that. The thing between her and Travis was tenuous and fleeting. The Nester and Hedley offer was concrete. It would last. She couldn't afford to make an illogical decision that would affect the rest of her life.

Caleb gazed at her for a long moment. "Okay. You're right. You know what's best for you. You do whatever you want."

She gave a rapid nod. "Thank you."

"I am sorry to lose you," he told her. "But I'm genuinely happy that you have this opportunity."

"You're an incredible man, Caleb Terrell." She meant it with all her heart.

# Nine

Caleb marched into Travis's living room, smacking his hands down on the back of a brown, leather armchair in obvious anger. "What in the hell did you do to her?"

Travis came to his feet. "Huh?" He did a double take of Caleb's icy expression. "You mean Danielle?"

"*Yes,* I mean Danielle."

"I didn't do a thing to her. She got ticked off and left."

"She was practically in tears. Do you have any idea what it takes to make Danielle cry?"

Guilt clenched Travis's stomach. Not that he'd done anything wrong. Randal was the bad guy here.

Travis was trying to help. "I told her the truth," he defended.

"What truth?"

"The truth about Randal Kleinfeld. Did she tell you she's taking the D.C. job?"

Caleb gave a sharp nod.

Travis felt his nostrils flare. "It's a mistake. A big mistake. This whole thing has been orchestrated by Randal Kleinfeld, and he's trying to get back with her. I warned her in Vegas, but she wouldn't listen. Oh, sure, later, when he showed his true colors, she admitted I was right. But does she remember that now? No. She thinks he'll back off. She thinks she can handle him. But he's pond-scum. He'll hurt her. And she can't be around him."

Caleb's expression had moderated. "Is that what you told her?"

"Not in so many words. I reminded her that he had ulterior motives."

Caleb moved around the armchair and sat down.

Travis followed suit on the sofa across from him. "Did you try to talk her out of it?" he asked.

Caleb shook his head. "It's her choice, her career. I can't hold her back."

"You wouldn't be holding her back," Travis pointed out. "You'd be saving her from a big mistake."

"It's a hugely prestigious law firm," said Caleb.

"One in which Randal is well and thoroughly entrenched. What do you think will happen if she refuses to date him? He'll get revenge. He'll try to undermine and discredit her. And he's the one with the contacts and relationships in D.C., not her."

"And if she does date him?" Caleb asked.

Travis felt his blood pressure go up a notch. The thought of Danielle in Randal's arms made him want to put his fist through a wall.

"That'll make it even worse," he told Caleb. "He'll trap her, and her entire world will be tangled up with that jerk."

Caleb was silent for a moment. "It's still her decision."

Travis gazed at his brother-in-law, grappling inside his head. He shouldn't say what he was about to say, but he had to say it.

He spoke softly. "You can stop her."

Caleb immediately refused. "No, I can't. And even if I could, I won't. I'm not going to guilt-trip her into staying with Milburn and Associates."

"Not Milburn and Associates." Travis had a better idea. "Active Equipment."

Caleb drew sharply back. "We're not a law firm."

Travis drummed his fingertips on the arm of the sofa, composing his arguments. "But you could use a staff lawyer. I've heard enough about the business to guess you could use Danielle full-time. Pantara and South America alone would keep her busy." He paused. "Make her an offer. Make it a good one. Keep her for yourself."

The grandfather clock ticked off seconds in the corner of the room. Travis could feel his heart beating in his chest. His body temperature rose a degree, and sweat began to form on his skin while he waited for Caleb's answer.

It was a full minute before Caleb spoke. "What's going on here, Travis?"

Travis knew he had to be honest with Caleb. "Randal can't have her. I can't let that happen."

"You want to keep her in Lyndon Valley."

"Yes."

"You want to keep her with you?"

Travis swallowed. He didn't understand why, and he didn't know how, but every instinct he possessed told him to keep her close and protect her. "Yes."

Caleb's hand rose to his chin, and his eyes took on a faraway look.

"What happened to all the fighting?" he finally asked.

"We still fight," Travis admitted.

Caleb seemed to digest that. "See, trouble is, I'm

not convinced you're not Active Equipment's very own Randal."

Travis nearly came out of his seat. "I'm not some pretentious fake. I'm not going to hurt Danielle. I am *nothing* like him."

"Can you swear to me you're looking out for her best interests?"

"Yes."

"That you're not going to hurt her?"

"Yes."

"You nearly made her cry already."

Travis did come to his feet. "That was over Randal. He's the only thing we fight about now. I like Danielle. I don't want her hurt. I don't want her stuck in D.C. with a scheming shyster who's out to get her." He drew a breath. "You know you want to keep her, Caleb. This is a perfect solution. It might not be exactly what she'd planned, but she could have a fantastic career with you. Active Equipment is going to be a global conglomerate. You're going to need people you trust. She's been with you since the beginning."

Caleb stood. "Seth isn't the only Jacobs who should have gone into politics."

"I'm not spinning you a story," Travis said with complete conviction.

"If you are, you're doing one heck of a good job."

Travis clamped his jaw to keep himself from over-selling the idea. He realized he cared more about Caleb's decision in this than he'd cared about anything in his life.

The silence stretched.

"I can offer," said Caleb.

A powerful rush of relief thudded through Travis.

"But I doubt she'll say yes."

"Convince her," said Travis with mounting enthusiasm.

"I'll lay out the facts, but that's all I can do."

"Offer a high salary, a good title, maybe vice president. Give her a bonus structure. Make sure you include dental. You've got dental at Active Equipment, right?"

"You want to take over on this?"

"No, no." Once again, Travis forced himself to stop talking.

"She'd be a valuable executive, and I have no problem making her a top offer. But I'm not a D.C. law firm, and that may be a deal breaker."

Travis forced himself to recognize the truth in Caleb's words. Danielle might not take the offer. There was nothing to indicate she'd even consider being a corporate lawyer. Truth was, there might not be a single thing he could do to keep her out of D.C.

\* \* \*

Danielle's bag was packed and waiting by the front door. She was in the office, putting the initial Pantara files in order for Caleb and whoever took her place. She needed to get back to Chicago today and give her notice in person before she called Nester and Hedley to accept their offer.

She'd transferred all of the attachments from her email account to Caleb's computer. She'd taken copies of her Pantara emails, and she'd filed all of her legal research by country. From what she could see so far, Pantara had some financial challenges, but nothing critical. What they seemed to be looking for from the merger was access to Active Equipment's customer base. It was becoming well known across international markets that Active Equipment was supplying superior products and top-notch after sales service to its clients in construction, resource extraction and heavy industry.

Satisfied that everything was well under control, Danielle closed her email box, shut down the file program, and rose from her desk chair. She lifted her bag, slipped it over her shoulder, and took a last look around the room.

It was a quirky, little office with a sloped ceiling and a small window overlooking the hay barn, the fields and mountains beyond. Danielle couldn't help but smile at the thought that she was likely the only lawyer at Milburn and Associates who had a view of cattle from her office window.

Crossing to the window, she experienced a bit of nostalgia, realizing she'd never see this particular view again. Though she and Caleb had formed a quasi-personal relationship over the years, she was under no illusion that they'd see each other socially.

She'd certainly never see Travis again. The thought brought a familiar ache to her chest. She knew it was crazy to feel this way, and she'd spent most of last night fighting it. She wasn't going to miss him, at least not long term. Theirs wasn't that kind of a relationship. Theirs wasn't a relationship at all.

Still, she was sorry they'd fought yesterday. In fact, when she woke up this morning, she'd been half tempted to go to him and apologize. He might have been belligerent and meddlesome, but she hadn't needed to lash out at him. He didn't know Randal the way she did. Randal wasn't going to be a problem.

In fact, after the few nights with Travis, she wouldn't be looking twice at Randal ever again. She knew the difference now between mediocre physical intimacy and true lovemaking. Travis had made love to her, and she'd never again settle for less.

"Danielle?" came Caleb's voice.

She turned to face him, banishing her melancholy thoughts and squaring her shoulders. Her decision was made, and it was time to move forward.

"Everything's filed," she told him. "It should be easy for someone else to take over." She moved toward him, determined to make this a professional, succinct goodbye. "But call me if you need anything, anything at all."

"Do you have a minute to talk?" he asked, his expression quite serious.

She paused. "Yes. Is something wrong?"

He gestured to the desk chair. "Nothing's wrong."

"Good." She hesitantly sat down, perching on the edge.

He braced his butt against a side table. "I'd like to make you an offer."

She waited a moment, trying to figure out where he was going. "An offer for what?"

"A job."

"You mean keep you as a client?" She had to be honest with him. "That'll depend on Nester and Hedley. But I'm not sure Active Equipment will fit in with my new portfolio. Of course, the firm overall would be thrilled to have you come over. But you might not be assigned to me."

"I wasn't talking about Nester and Hedley."

"Oh." Then she was stumped.

"I want you to work for Active Equipment. Full-time. As a corporate attorney. Your title will be Vice President of International Affairs."

Danielle slumped back in the chair, blinking at Caleb in confusion. "Uh, could you repeat that?"

"Vice President of International Affairs."

"I don't understand."

He cocked his head sideways and smiled. "I don't want to lose you. You know as well as I do how far we've come, how much potential we have going forward. I need smart people around me that I can trust. You're an incredibly smart person, and I know I can trust you. Money won't be a problem, you can name your price. And we have dental."

Danielle gave a helpless laugh. "Dental?"

"Does that sweeten the pot for you?"

"I still don't understand." She'd never thought of any career path other than a law firm. She didn't understand what Caleb meant by Vice President of International Affairs.

"You'd be doing all the things you do for Active Equipment already, plus, well plus whatever else you want to do. I know you, Danielle. I can point you in a general direction, and you'll figure out how to help me." He braced his hands on either side of the table. "You said yourself you weren't looking to leave Chicago, that the Nester and Hedley offer had come out of the blue. Well, here's another out of the blue offer for you. I hope it's something you'll consider."

She didn't have the first idea of how to respond. She loved working with Caleb, with Active Equipment. She was certain they had a huge future ahead of them. But to abandon her entire career plan, to take a complete left turn like that? How could a person make that decision?

"I'm already packed," she told him, realizing how silly it sounded even as the words came out. Who cared about an overnight bag down in his foyer?

"Do you have any questions?"

"I don't know. My brain seems to have shut down."

Caleb laughed. "I'm torn between telling you to go away and think about it and giving you a thorough sales pitch right here and now."

"I have a flight booked to Chicago," she pointed out, glancing at her watch.

"I have an airplane," he countered.

Her mind ticked through the possibilities. She could stay in Chicago, take on a whole, new exciting venture, and she wouldn't have Randal to worry about. She wouldn't be the new person on the totem pole. She'd have flexibility, autonomy.

The sky was the limit for Active Equipment. And, *and,* if she did want to move to a law firm at some point in the future, a vice president position at an international conglomerate would look very good on her resume.

And then there was Travis. She'd be in Chicago, but she'd still have her connection to Lyndon Valley. She was certain she'd be back, possibly often. Intellectually, she knew that was probably a bad thing. But emotionally, she wasn't ready to let him go. If she said yes to Caleb, she'd get to see Travis again.

For a second, she heard her mother's voice inside her head, warning her to never, never, *ever* make a career decision based on a man. But she shoved it away. It was a good job offer. It was a great job offer. Travis was incidental. She'd make certain he stayed incidental.

"I feel like I should negotiate something," she told Caleb.

A grin stretched across his face. "There's nothing to negotiate. Just tell me what it'll take."

"You're just going to hand me a vice presidency, on a silver platter?"

"You've earned it."

"I'm not sure about that."

"Well, I'm sure about that. And I'm the one who counts."

Danielle grinned.

Caleb came to his feet. "What do you say?"

She rose. "I think you've just made me an offer I can't refuse."

Caleb stuck out his square, callused hand. "That was my plan."

She reached out to shake it.

His expression was warm, his tone deep and sincere. "Welcome aboard, Danielle."

It took Danielle a week to clear things up at Milburn and Associates. She would have stayed longer, but they were clearly annoyed with her for leaving, doubly annoyed at losing Active Equipment as a client, and things in the office were tense. By midmorning Friday, she was walking out the door. By noon, she was on the corporate jet winging her way back to Lyndon City to meet Caleb.

She struggled not to think about Travis, but the closer they got to Lyndon Valley, the more he was on her mind. She hadn't spoken to him since their fight, and she couldn't help but wonder how he'd reacted to the news that she'd be working for his brother instead of going to D.C. He hadn't wanted her to take the job in D.C., but that didn't mean he wanted her underfoot, either.

Part of her wanted to avoid him. The other part

wanted to get the first meeting over with as soon as possible. At least once she saw him she'd know where things stood. Whatever it was, she promised herself she could handle it. She'd have to handle it. She'd closed all the other career doors in her life, and her professional future was with Active Equipment. She was absolutely determined to succeed.

Caleb met her at the small airport, stowing her suitcase into the canopy of the pickup truck.

"Glad to have you with us," he offered, opening the passenger door.

She smiled, genuinely happy. Now that she was here, everything felt right. She grasped the door handle and hauled herself into the cab, smoothing her short skirt beneath her on the plaid-covered bench seat.

"Nester and Hedley would have sent a limo," she couldn't help but tease.

"We'd break an axle in the potholes," he retorted, clearly not the least bit offended or apologetic.

"I can see I'm going to have to adjust my standards."

"I don't think you'll have any trouble." He closed the door to round the hood.

She glanced down at her straight, black skirt, the white blouse and the blazer that she'd worn out of habit. If Caleb was going to need her in Lyndon Valley very often, she'd have to rethink the wardrobe.

"I may have to invest in a pair of plain ol' blue jeans," she told him as he opened the driver's door.

"Co-op's open 'till nine."

Danielle laughed. "That would be a first."

"Twenty bucks a pair. You can buy two."

She could buy five. Her blazer alone had cost four hundred dollars.

"But not today," said Caleb, slamming the door and hitting the key to start the engine.

"What's today?"

"Rehearsal dinner tonight."

"Rehearsal dinner?" Then it dawned on her. "Lisa and Alex's wedding?"

"Is tomorrow." Caleb confirmed as he pulled the shifter into reverse and backed out of the gravel parking spot.

She glanced at her watch. It was after two. "Do you have time to take me all the way to the ranch?" She didn't understand how he was going to make it back for the dinner.

"We're not going to the ranch."

"A hotel?"

That wasn't a problem. She could set up shop in a hotel room for the weekend. Maybe she would shop around for some more casual clothes.

"We're staying at the mayor's mansion."

"What do you mean 'we'?" Danielle wasn't involved in the wedding.

"Everyone's there for the weekend."

Everyone would most certainly include Travis. Danielle's mouth went dry. "You can drop me off at a hotel."

"What?"

"Caleb, I don't want to be in the way." And she didn't want to see Travis.

She'd thought she did. She'd thought the best thing was to get it over with. But she'd changed her mind. She wanted to put it off as long as possible. She very much feared he was holding a grudge. While she couldn't stop thinking about how much she liked him.

"You're not going to be in the way," said Caleb. "The place is huge."

"Square footage isn't my worry. This is a very special occasion for your family."

"They're pretty excited," Caleb agreed as he slowed down, entering the city limits.

"They'll be too busy to worry about me."

He sent her an arched look. "What makes you think they're going to worry about you? They'll park you in a bedroom, and you'll blend with the crowd. Katrina can't wait to see you."

Danielle gave an involuntary smile at the thought of hanging out with Katrina again.

"Fine," she agreed. She'd simply make sure she stayed out of everyone's path, especially Travis's.

"You say that as if you had a choice."

Danielle twisted her body to give him a mock scowl. "Are you going to be some kind of autocratic boss?"

He glanced at her. "You have a problem with that?"

She huffed a little. "You might find yourself with a rebellious employee."

His lips stretched into a grin. "I can live with that."

He flipped on his signal and pulled into the palatial driveway of the mayor's mansion.

The lawns were fine trimmed, as were the hedges. The building itself was three stories high. A huge front porch greeted them, with white pillars and an ornate rail.

Danielle took a deep breath, steeling her nerves.

Her next meeting with Travis was likely only moments away.

Travis watched from an archway leading to the great room while Katrina squealed and gave Danielle a tight hug. Then it was Lisa's turn, then Mandy and finally Abigail. His arms felt ridiculously empty and she hadn't even looked his way.

"You're coming to the dinner, right?" Lisa asked her. "And to the wedding."

Danielle glanced momentarily to Caleb then back to Lisa. "I'm… Uh… No. I have work to do. But it's very kind of you to ask."

"Don't be silly." Lisa grabbed her hands. "You have to come."

"Absolutely, she'll come," Katrina put in. "It's a wedding. And there's no way we're leaving you here all by yourself while we go out and party tonight."

Danielle shook her head. "I really can't intrude. It's your family."

"You're family now."

"I'm an employee," Danielle corrected. "Just because I happen to be here working—"

"Don't insult us," said Mandy.

Danielle turned to her in obvious astonishment.

"Caleb thinks of you as much more than an employee. We all do."

"But—"

"Please come," said Lisa in a cajoling voice. "It would make me happy to have you there. And I'm the bride. You can't say no to the bride."

Danielle glanced to Caleb again, clearly uncertain about what to do.

"I don't need you to work on anything tonight," he told her with conviction.

"I don't have anything suitable to wear to a wedding," she protested, gesturing to her rather severe suit. "It's all like this."

"We'll go shopping," Katrina piped up.

"You've got work to do, young lady," Abigail reminded her. "Decorating committee. All of us."

Katrina gave a pretty pout.

Travis stepped forward. "I'll take her shopping."

The five women, along with Caleb, swung their gazes toward him.

"You?" asked Katrina in obvious astonishment. "Going dress shopping?"

"I'm not decorating," he pointed out. He didn't give a damn what errand got him alone with Danielle, so long as he got there.

He looked at her, struggling to keep his tone and expression neutral. "What do you say? Make the bride happy?"

"I'm—"

"I suppose you could drive her to the mall," Katrina put in. "But you have to send me a picture of each dress so I can help choose."

"You don't trust my taste?" Travis asked her.

"Why on earth would I trust your taste?"

"I'll send photos," Travis promised, making a show of looking at his watch. "But we'd better get going."

Before Danielle had a chance to protest, he paced across the room and took her arm, gently turning her and urging her toward the front door.

Caleb shot him a knowing smirk as he passed by, but Travis ignored him.

"Rehearsal at six. Dinner's at seven," Lisa called from behind.

Travis gave them all a wave over his head. "We'll be back in plenty of time."

Then he pushed open the front door, and suddenly he and Danielle were alone. He had no idea what to say.

"What just happened?" she asked, glancing over her shoulder in confusion as they walked toward the wide staircase.

"You've been bamboozled by the Jacobs family."

"But why?"

He shrugged, pulling his truck keys out of his pocket. "Lisa wants you at the wedding. Really, Danielle, there was no chance they'd leave you home alone tonight."

"I offered to stay at a hotel."

Her words gave him a little jolt. He didn't want

her at a hotel. He wanted her here, with him, where he could talk to her, look at her, listen to her breathe. He realized he had it bad for her, but he couldn't fight it. All he'd done for the past week was miss her. If he hadn't known she was coming back to work for Caleb, he might have gone stark raving mad.

He opened the pickup door for her, offering his hand to help her up to the seat. "Nobody wants you to stay at a hotel."

She ignored his hand and hoisted herself up to the seat. "I feel like an interloper."

"You're not an interloper. So stop worrying."

With her settled, he moved to the driver's seat. It was only a couple of miles to the Springroad Mall. He knew Abigail's favorite store was Blooms.

Once on the road, the silence settled between them, and he could feel the tension ramping up. Danielle tugged her skirt an inch down her thigh. Then she smoothed back her hair then tapped her fingertips against her knee.

Travis turned on the radio, filling the cab with a country ballad about lost love. He immediately wished he hadn't done it.

"It ought to be sunny for the wedding tomorrow," he noted out of desperation.

She didn't respond.

"They're having the wedding in the garden." He paused. "Reception in the mansion."

"I'm sorry," she blurted out.

He was confused. "About the wedding?"

"No. About the last time we spoke. I shouldn't have stormed out on you. You were out of line, and I was angry, but I could have handled it better."

He was so surprised by her unexpected words, that he didn't know what to say.

She was silent, then she adjusted her seat belt. Then she moved her sun visor.

He finally came up with, "I didn't expect you to apologize."

"I kind of expected you would."

Okay, that was even more surprising. "Me? What for?"

He'd only stated the facts.

"What for?" Her voice went a notch higher. "For meddling in my life."

"That wasn't meddling. That was warning you about someone who was operating against you."

"I told you I could deal with Randal."

"You don't have to deal with him anymore." And *that* was thanks to Travis. Though he'd never let on.

"I know that. But, I could have. And I would have. And you need to keep your opinions to yourself."

Travis thought about it for a moment. "I don't really see that happening."

She pressed her lips together. "At least keep your opinions about *my* life to yourself."

He shook his head. "Seems unlikely."

"Am I going to have to avoid you?"

"Personally, I'd suggest you get used to hearing my opinions. It'll be a whole lot easier than avoiding me."

*"Travis,"* she protested.

"I mean, take a look at us now." He swung the truck into the parking lot of the Springroad Mall. "You're in town fifteen minutes, and already we're together.

"That's your fault," she accused.

"It is," he agreed. He'd shamelessly manipulated himself into this position. "But it shows you how easily it's going to happen."

He brought the truck to a halt, and they both climbed out of the vehicle.

"I thought things might have changed," she told him as they crossed the parking lot.

"What things?"

"You and me. Our relationship."

Her words took him by surprise. Did the woman have amnesia? "I'd say our relationship has changed a whole lot."

"Not fundamentally."

"Yes, fundamentally."

"You're still the same. I'm still the same. We can't seem to help from rubbing each other the wrong way."

It was on the tip of his tongue to make a joke about all the times when they'd rubbed each other exactly the *right* way. But he kept silent.

"Let's find you a dress," he said instead, nodding to a large purple sign on the side of the mall. "Abigail seems to like Blooms."

"I'm sure it's fine," said Danielle, sounding like she was heading for the executioner.

He opened the glass door. "You might want to work up a little enthusiasm. It's an important wedding, and I'm buying."

"Oh, no, you're not."

"I got you into this."

"Caleb got me into this. I asked him to drop me off at a hotel."

"Everyone would have been disappointed if he'd done that."

Travis included himself in everyone. Even now, sparring with her, frustrating her, on the receiving end of nothing but her annoyance, he was incredibly glad she was here. He realized he'd rather be arguing with Danielle than doing anything else with any other woman.

She gave an exaggerated sigh. "I wouldn't have been disappointed."

He nudged her shoulder. "Cowboy up. This isn't the end of the world."

"Cowboy up? I'm dress shopping here."

"It's a versatile metaphor. It means quit whining and get 'er done."

"I know what it means."

They passed through the big doorway to Blooms, and she stopped in front of a display of dresses.

"So, are you going to do it?" he asked.

She squared her shoulders, reaching for a simple, gray cocktail dress. "I'm going to do it. I'll buy myself a dress, say happy things to the bride and groom and cheerfully chat my way through dinner."

"It's a tough life," Travis deadpanned.

"Shut up."

"I don't think Katrina is going to like the gray." He extracted his phone from his jeans pocket and turned on the camera. He wasn't crazy about gray, either. He hoped he could talk Danielle into something sexier.

# Ten

Danielle pulled the curtain shut on the changing cubical, and hung three dresses on the hooks placed around it, dropping her purse on the chair. She hadn't been crazy about the gray dress, either. She might have mixed emotions about attending Lisa's wedding. But if she was going to be there, she wanted to help celebrate, not bring anyone down with such a somber color.

She stripped out of her suit and pulled on a knee-length, aqua party dress. It had cap sleeves and multi-layered, gauze skirt. It was pretty, but seemed a bit young and frivolous for the occasion.

"Let's see," came Travis's voice through the curtain.

"I don't like it," she called back.

"I need to take a picture."

Danielle rolled her eyes in the mirror.

"Katrina's texting me," he said.

Danielle decided it was easier to humor Katrina than fight with her. "Fine." She drew back the curtain.

"Come out," Travis instructed.

Danielle took a few steps forward.

He raised the camera and snapped a shot. "Turn around."

She felt incredibly self-conscious under his scrutiny. "This is ridiculous."

"Tell that to Katrina."

Danielle reluctantly turned around. She posed for only a moment, then she retreated back into the changing room.

She didn't like having Travis stare at her. Okay, actually she did like having Travis stare at her. And that was the problem. There was nothing about a fashion show that ought to have been sexy, but she was getting aroused anyway. It was embarrassing.

She switched to the next dress, determined to get this over with as quickly as possible. The silk fabric was soft against her skin. It draped over one shoulder, with a wide, sash belt. She'd forgotten to remove her bra, so she had to take off the dress and try again.

"Ready?" called Travis.

Standing there in nothing but her panties, Danielle's chest tightened, and her skin flushed in reaction to the mere sound of his voice.

"Just a sec," she called out a little breathlessly.

She pulled the moss-green silk over her near naked body, reaching around to zip up the back. When she turned, she nearly groaned in despair. Her nipples had hardened and were clearly visible through the fabric. There was no way she was leaving this room.

"Danielle?" he called.

"It's definitely a no-go."

"Let's see."

"Not this one."

"Come on. Katrina is waiting. She gave a thumb's down to the blue one."

"No kidding." Danielle glanced back into the mirror. Okay. Her body had calmed down a little. She could risk it.

She pulled back the curtain, walking out on the carpet.

"Not bad," said Travis.

"Really? You're a fashion critic, too?"

He snapped a picture. "I know what I like on women."

"What you like on women has no bearing on my decision here."

He swirled his finger, indicating she should turn around. "Probably a good thing. If I had my way, you'd be—"

"Don't you dare say something indecent." She turned back.

He grinned unrepentantly. Then his gaze dropped to her breasts and stayed there.

Uh-oh.

"Next," she quickly stated, whirling to get back into the changing room.

The third dress was a muted, Carolina blue. It was rich satin, with a strapless, tucked, crisscross bodice. Tiny crystals at the waist and neckline gave a muted sparkle, while the full skirt draped softly over a subtle crinoline, ending just above her knees.

"Katrina says no again," Travis called.

"Your sister has good taste," Danielle called back.

She craned her neck to look at the back of the dress, straightening the neckline, then she took in the side view. It wasn't bad at all. She'd have to pick up some dangling earrings, but her neutral pumps would work with it.

She opened the curtain and stepped out.

Travis stood still and stared.

"What do you think?" She pirouetted.

He stepped closer then closer still, until he was almost touching her. She caught her breath.

"You're going to dance with me, right?"

"That's not an option."

"Oh, yes, it is."

"Travis."

His broad hand covered hers. "Listen, we can pretend all day long, but there's something between us. And it's not going away. Dancing with you is the very least I want to do."

His blue eyes were intense while they held her gaze. His hand was warm on hers, his scent surrounding her, reminding her of things she'd hoped to forget. But she remembered in vivid detail, and her pulse leaped, her humming arousal gathered strength.

"I'll dance with you," she told him.

He smiled, and his hand tightened around hers.

"But that's all I'm promising."

"That's all I'm asking."

She hesitated for a moment. "You like the dress?"

His voice went husky. "I like the dress. I like what's inside the dress. I'm going to love the whole package when we're dancing together."

"Travis," she sighed this time. She knew she

should make him stop flirting, but her protest was only halfhearted.

"I'm very glad you're not in D.C."

She grabbed the opportunity to tone things down. "I think it's going to work out with Caleb."

Travis opened his mouth, but then closed it again without speaking.

"You should take a picture for Katrina," Danielle prompted.

"I don't really care what she says."

"I thought we were humoring her."

"Okay." He took a step back. "Smile."

Danielle turned and paused for a second picture. Then she made her way back into the change room.

"I'm going to need some earrings," she called as she finished putting her own clothes back on.

"Katrina likes it," came Travis's response.

"That's good."

Danielle slung her purse over her shoulder and hung the dress over her arm, sliding back the curtain to exit.

"Do you mind if we look for earrings?" she asked him.

"Not at all. You want me to carry that?"

"You don't have to be my assistant." Danielle had never met a man eager to trail after a woman in a dress shop lugging around her purchases.

"I'm a gentleman." He removed the sparkly dress from her arm and draped it over his own.

"You're not at all insecure about your masculinity, are you?"

"You can't get more macho than bull riding."

She glanced around at the dozens of shoppers. "Nobody here knows you ride bulls."

"We're in Lyndon City, Danielle. Everybody here knows I ride bulls."

"So, the real test is if you're willing to follow me around shopping in Chicago."

"Bring it on, sweetheart."

Her heart skipped a beat at the endearment. Luckily, she didn't need to respond, because they'd arrived at the jewelry section of the store. She quickly veered away from him, zeroing in on an earring display.

She moved her way past the studs and hoops. She needed something with a drop. When she came to the right section, she concentrated on the display beneath the glass, refusing to look back at Travis.

A pair quickly caught her eye. They were white gold, in a twisted vine pattern, decorated with white sapphires and aquamarines. She asked the clerk to see them and held them up to her ears in front of a small mirror on the countertop. They were perfect.

"Find something?" asked Travis from a few counters away.

"I did."

"You're pretty fast at this."

"You go shopping with a lot of women, do you?" she asked as she moved toward him.

"Occasionally. I do have three sisters. Though, Mandy's in and out in about thirty seconds."

"You find something for yourself?" Danielle teased, glancing down at the display. To her surprise, it was diamond rings.

He pointed. "That one looks like Lisa's. She went with colored diamonds. Mandy's is classic, a solitaire. Katrina's is really modern." He pointed to a platinum, nonsymmetric swirl with varying sizes of diamonds decorating it. "Reed bought it at some fancy store in New York. I can't even imagine the price tag."

"Are you doing a study of engagement rings?"

"Just thinking about the differences between the Jacobs women. Abigail has an heirloom ring from Craig Mountain Castle."

"That sounds nice."

He studied the display case in silence for a moment.

"Do you have a favorite?" she asked him.

"Favorite sister?"

She nudged him with her elbow. "Ring."

He shook his head. "You?"

They all looked beautiful to her. "I've never given it a lot of thought. My family's focus was more on the prenup than anything else."

Travis chuckled.

"I think," she ventured in all honesty. "The ring's a bit irrelevant. I'd be a lot more interested in the man presenting it."

"Good answer."

The clerk appeared in front of them. "Can I help you with something?"

Danielle and Travis glanced rather guiltily at one another, both obviously realizing how this looked.

"Un, no," she quickly answered. "We have a friend who's getting married."

It wasn't really much of an explanation, but she quickly rattled on. "I'm ready to pay, if you could direct me…"

"Right over here," she pointed to a nearby register. "I'll be happy to ring those through for you."

Danielle ducked her head and quickly followed the middle-aged woman. What was the matter with her? She needed to put up barriers against Travis, not engage in cozy chats over diamond rings of all things.

* * *

There were a whole lot of people at the rehearsal in the garden of the mayor's mansion. Danielle stood off to one side, trying to stay in the background. She had been introduced to the Jacobses' parents, Hugo and Maureen. Lisa was the daughter of Maureen's deceased sister Nicole. Nicole had run away from home as a teenager, and the family had only recently learned of her daughter's existence.

Danielle had met Abigail Jacobs on several occasions. Her husband, Zach, had grown up with the groom, Alex, in a home for orphaned boys. She was also already acquainted with Niki Gerrard, Caleb and Reed's half sister. Niki had recently married Washington, D.C. mover and shaker Sawyer Layton. The two now spent as much time as they could on their own ranch in Lyndon Valley.

Abigail was the matron of honor, while Zach served as best man. Katrina and Mandy were bridesmaids. Two of Alex's longtime friends from DFB Brewery were standing up as groomsmen. Danielle couldn't immediately remember their names. Nor could she remember the names of their girlfriends. Seth, as mayor, was officiating, right now directing operations for the rehearsal. His new wife, Darby, was clearly pivotal in the organization of the event.

"You okay?" Travis's voice so close startled her.

"I'm fine," she answered.

"You look worried."

"I'm just trying to keep everyone straight."

"I could write up a cheat sheet."

"That would be nice. Did I ever mention I'm an only child? When I get married, *if* I get married, there will be approximately six people in attendance."

"I doubt that."

But Danielle gave a decisive nod. "There'll be no need at all for a cheat sheet."

"Wait until you see all this tomorrow."

"I'm dreading it."

"Don't be modest. You're in crowds all the time. Look at the conference in Vegas. I've seen you work a room."

"With lawyers," she protested. "I can talk business all day long, but put me in a family setting." She gave a shiver. "I pretty much panic."

"I'm a lowly cowboy, and I braved your lawyers' Van Ostram Gardens for you."

"Lowly cowboy, *huh*," she mocked. "You fit in anywhere."

"So do you."

Seth called out to Darby, who gave a saucy answer while moving the bridesmaids into position for the mock procession. Everyone erupted in laughter.

"Holidays at my house were sedate and boring," said Danielle. "Nobody teased, nobody joked. We dressed impeccably, and discussed meritorious topics of international interest, while staff served fine French cuisine."

"Sounds horrifying," Travis remarked.

"My point is that my upbringing was very different from yours, and this massive family thing is intimidating."

"Holidays at our house were bedlam and chaos."

"I bet you loved it."

"I loved it," he agreed.

A sense of emptiness overshadowed Danielle's feelings.

Hugo was giving Lisa away, putting her hand in Alex's, who gazed down at her with love and longing. She tried to imagine her own father walking her down the aisle, shaking the hand of her soon to be husband. The picture didn't work.

He'd probably wax on about the archaic convention of a woman passing from her father's care to her husband's. Danielle could take care of herself, she didn't need to count on any man. By the way, did she need him to look over her prenup?

A spurt of laughter erupted from her.

"What?" asked Travis.

"Nothing. Will you really help me?"

"Help you what?"

"Navigate your family tonight?"

There was a very slight pause before he answered.

"Yeah." His voice was husky, and the back of his hand brushed lightly against hers.

A spurt of desire in her abdomen was followed by a warm glow moving up her arm. She almost curled her hand into his palm, stopping herself just in time.

"That's a wrap," called Seth. "I think we've got it under control."

His wife, Darby, whispered something in his ear.

He grinned and immediately wrapped an arm around her, giving her a kiss on the temple.

"The cars will be waiting out front," he called to everyone else.

Chatting happily, the crowd started along the concrete pathway to the back of the mansion.

"Big breath," Travis whispered to Danielle as they both moved to follow.

They traveled in the same car, and Travis sat next to her at one of five round tables set up in the private, second-story room of the Riverfront Grill. It had an expansive view of the Lyndon River, looking west over the Rockies, and they were just in time for a gorgeous sunset.

Caleb and Mandy, along with Katrina and Reed, had joined them at the table. Alex and Lisa sat with Zach and Abigail at the head table, along with Hugo and Maureen. Danielle noticed that Maureen stuck fast to Lisa, taking every opportunity to hug her or smooth her hair. Both women glowed, seeming delighted in each other's company.

As Katrina chatted happily about the wedding cake, the flowers and the decorations they'd put up at the mansion during the afternoon, Danielle began to relax. Katrina raved about Danielle's dress, sharing the pictures with Mandy, and teasing Travis about being a shopping companion. Caleb and Reed stepped in as well, but Travis took it all in stride.

They were interrupted by the clinking of a knife against a glass. The room went silent, as Hugo rose to his feet.

Though he'd suffered a stroke many months back, he was now fully recovered. He looked strong and sure standing in front of his family.

"This is the time," he opened in a clear voice, "a toast would traditionally be given by the father of the bride." He looked to Lisa and smiled lovingly. "As you all know, these are special circumstances."

He paused and cleared his throat. "What I'm

about to say to you, I've discussed at length with your mother, with my wife Maureen."

Maureen reached up from her chair and took his hand, gripping it tight.

"I spoke with Lisa this morning. She and Alex have asked me to tell you this." Hugo paused again, clearly bracing himself.

Everyone in the room had gone still and silent.

"As you all know, we learned of Lisa, your cousin's, existence only recently. Her mother Nicole was an amazing young woman, who we miss and mourn every day. What you don't know, is for a short time, many, many years ago, Maureen and I grew apart in our marriage. We separated, even considered divorce."

Danielle felt Travis stiffen beside her. She glanced at his profile, seeing his jaw tighten and his eyes go hard.

"During that time, I had a short-lived relationship with Nicole. It ended amicably. She moved on, and I thought it was merely a blip on the radar of our lives." Hugo reached for a glass of water and took a drink.

Maureen reached up with her other hand, wrapping them both around his. Lisa was blinking rapidly, while Alex had placed an arm around her.

Danielle, along with everyone else in the room

could guess where this was going. She reflexively reached for Travis's hand. It was cold against hers, but she held on.

"Seth, Travis, Abigail, Mandy, Katrina." Hugo named each of his children individually. "Lisa is not just your cousin. She is your sister."

It was Hugo's turn to blink, but he couldn't quite contain his emotion, and a single tear streaked down his wrinkled face. He turned to the wedding couple. "And so, as the father of the bride, it is my proud and incredible honor to congratulate Alex, and tell you, Lisa, that I love you very much, that Maureen and I both loved your mother, and we could not be more delighted to have you as part of our family." He raised his glass. "To the beautiful bride."

There was only stunned silence, and then applause filled the room. Katrina squealed and jumped to her feet, rushing to Lisa to hug her tight. Mandy followed after her.

Maureen came to her feet and hugged Hugo, the two embracing for a long time.

Travis didn't move. He looked as if he'd been sucker punched.

Danielle leaned in, pressing herself against his shoulder. "Go," she whispered. "Lisa needs you right now."

Travis turned to stare blankly at Danielle.

"Go," she repeated, giving him a small shake. "Tell your sister you love her. Anything else can wait."

He seemed to rouse himself. Then he nodded his agreement.

He rose from his chair and strode determinedly to the head table. His eyes were warm, and his smile was genuine as he spoke to Lisa. He hugged her to his chest, then he shook Alex's hand. That he didn't speak to his father seemed lost in the general chaos surrounding the family.

"Looks like the women are taking it better than Travis and Seth," Caleb muttered.

Danielle scanned the room for Seth and realized Caleb was right. Seth was hugging his mother. Over her shoulder, his expression went tight and accusatory for the fleeting second that he met his father's eyes.

Danielle quickly switched her attention to Caleb. "I shouldn't be here." It wasn't right that she was witnessing this intimate family moment.

"Travis wants you here," said Caleb, causing Reed to send him a confused look.

"He wanted to dance with me," said Danielle. "He had no idea this was going to happen."

"It's good that you're here," Caleb insisted.

Katrina returned to the table, wrapping her arms around Reed's neck. "Isn't it wonderful?"

"It's a surprise," Reed responded.

"A good surprise. A *great* surprise."

"Well, well, well," said Mandy as she took her seat next to Caleb.

"People are complicated," said Caleb, lifting her hand and kissing her knuckles.

Travis plunked down. "Is *that* the word we're using?"

The tension was clear in his tone, and Mandy and Katrina both gaped at him.

"I think it's the right word," Danielle quickly put in. "Life doesn't come in a neat package with a bow on top."

He gave her a hard look. "That doesn't mean it—"

She grasped his shoulder, pulling up to kiss him hard on the lips. He stilled in what had to be shock. She pulled back a mere inch from his face.

"Shut up," she whispered harshly for his ears alone. "Don't hurt your sisters. Don't upset your family. Just shut up right now."

He didn't answer, but he leaned in and kissed her again, this time longer, and he was obviously no longer shocked.

They drew apart to amazed stares of everyone at the table.

"Danielle and I dated in Vegas," Travis told them all, his tone back to normal. "So, you might want to get used to her kissing me."

"You dated in Vegas?" asked Katrina.

"We had lunch," said Danielle. "You know we danced that night. I wouldn't exactly call it—"

"Dating," said Travis with finality, and he looped an arm around her shoulders.

"Well, well, well," Mandy repeated.

Reed stepped in, reaching for one of two bottles in the center of the table. "I think I should pour the wine."

"Excellent idea," said Caleb.

Danielle swiftly lifted her glass and held it out. She had no idea what was going to happen next, but a little wine sure couldn't hurt the situation.

Seth joined Travis where he'd parked himself against the wall, gazing through the window at the lights on the river walk below.

Seth copied his posture, leaning back, staring out the window. "You as ticked at him as I am?"

"Yeah. For a minute there I wanted to string him up."

"He cheated on our mother," said Seth, downing a final swallow of whiskey.

Travis wished he had one himself. "She didn't deserve that."

"They *were* separated, I suppose."

"Do you have any memory of that?" Travis asked his brother. "I don't remember any fights, any trouble. Did it all just go away?"

"I have a vague recollection of yelling, of Mom telling him to leave, crying. She was hugging you, and Abigail was in the bassinet. I think I picked her up and brought her to Mom."

Seth tried to take another drink, but the glass was empty. "Weird, huh? That memory shimmering there all this time?"

"He shouldn't get off scot-free."

"It seems like Mom's forgiven him."

"She loves him," said Travis. His mother was kind, caring and pragmatic. Just because she'd given their father a break, doesn't mean he deserved it.

"We love him, too," Seth reminded his brother.

Travis wanted to argue the point. They loved the man they'd thought he was. This was a whole new side of him.

"What are you going to do?" he asked Seth instead.

"Nothin'. It was a long time ago, and it brought us Lisa. It's up to Mom to forgive him or not. And it seems like she has."

Travis thought about that. "With you and Darby. Would you ever, I mean even if you were fighting, would you cheat on her?"

Seth's gaze moved to Darby. "Not even with a gun to my head."

"Good to know." Somehow that reaffirmed Travis's faith in his gender. "Caleb and Reed, do you think? 'Cause I might have to kill them if they hurt our sisters."

Seth grinned. "Not a chance. Not Zach, either. Despite what you hear, bro, most men don't cheat. We marry the right person, and we stop wanting anyone else."

Travis's gaze fell on Danielle, laughing and talking with Katrina. He thought he understood what Seth meant. He wasn't married to Danielle, wasn't in love with her, but when she was around, the entire world disappeared. Other women were irrelevant.

"Thanks," he told his brother, straightening away from the wall.

"What are you going to do?" asked Seth.

"Nothin'," Travis tossed over his shoulder.

His brother was right. Their father and Nicole were the past. Lisa was the present.

He reached Danielle. "Hey."

She turned and smiled at him, and he felt its impact right to his toes.

"You want to walk?" he asked on impulse.

"Walk where?"

"Back to the mansion. We can cut across the park."

She glanced down at her shoes, which were heels but not too high. "Sure."

"See you guys back there," sang Katrina, taking her leave.

Travis slipped his hand over Danielle's, and they took the back exit, climbing down a narrow staircase to come out at the river walk.

"You okay?" she asked as they set a course along the bank, the sound of the river filling in the background.

"I'm okay. I talked to Seth."

"Did you talk to your dad?"

"Not yet. But I will. I don't like it. I'm not sure my mother should forgive him. But that's not my call to make."

*"Really."* She seemed surprised.

"What really?"

"I know you meddle. And I always heard you were a hothead."

"I am a hothead."

"That was a sound, reasoned, rational decision."

"I have my moments."

"That, you do," she agreed as they walked.

"You're the hothead," he accused.

"I most certainly am not."

"You kissed me to shut me up. Was that reasoned and rational?"

"No, that was impulsive. But you were about to do something really stupid."

"Impulsive is another way of saying hothead."

"I notice you don't disagree on the stupid part."

He tugged her playfully against his arm, and she hop-skipped to keep her balance.

"I don't disagree on the stupid part," he told her.

"That's progress."

"Progress toward what?"

She shrugged her slim shoulders. "I don't know."

They walked in silence for a while, along the river, then across the park walkway. Travis kept her hand in his, glancing every once in a while at her profile, reminding himself how beautiful she was, how smart, how funny. He was content simply to be with her, and he wished the walk would never end.

Too soon, they arrived at the back gate of the mansion and its gardens.

"What now?" asked Danielle, taking in the arched wrought iron.

"I've got the combination," he told her, typing

into the key pad. The lock clicked free, and he pulled the gate back wide enough to allow them to go through.

"Impressive," she said as she passed.

"You mock my bull riding, but this does it for you?"

"Bull riding is brute strength, no thinking required. This shows preplanning and intelligence."

"I've never met a foolish bull rider," Travis defended.

"I bet you've met a lot of bruised ones."

"True enough."

"Why would an intelligent man get on the back of a two-thousand-pound beast intent on doing him harm?"

"The adrenaline rush," answered Travis, pulling the gate back into place. "You can't beat it for a thrill."

She'd stopped to wait. So they were now facing each other in the dark garden.

"You like thrills, cowboy?"

He heard a sensual edge to the question, but he was sure it was his own imagination.

"I love thrills." He wanted to kiss her so badly, it was all he could do to hold back.

She was drop-dead gorgeous in the moonlight.

Her hair was mussed, her lips dark, her eyes soft pools above beautifully flushed cheeks.

"I like safety and predictability," she countered.

He raised his fingertips to her chin. "That's too bad."

"Why?" she asked in a voice that had gone low.

"Because I'm not predictable, and I'm sure not safe."

His lips parted, but she didn't reply.

"I'm going to kiss you, Danielle," he warned.

"I know," she acknowledged.

"And I'm not going to stop."

# Eleven

Danielle let herself mold against Travis's body, holding herself tight against his hard strength. She hadn't known until now just how much she'd missed him, how much she'd ached for his touch, his taste, his scent. There was nothing reasonable or rational about her emotions, but she felt as if she'd finally come home.

She kissed him deeply, instantly opening up to him as his tongue tangled with hers. His hand slipped its way down her back, cupping her buttocks, pulling her tight to the vee of his thighs. She twined her arms around his neck, stretching up to devour his kisses.

Her skin felt too tight, warm and restless. At the

same time, desire swirled from the base of her belly to the tops of her thighs, circling, tightening every nerve ending it found. The breeze buffeted her ears, muting sounds and blocking out the world. There was only Travis, nothing but Travis.

Their kisses went on and on.

"I've missed you," Travis groaned against her mouth. "I've missed you so, so much."

"Don't let me go," she begged. She couldn't stand it if something broke them apart right now.

"I'm not letting you go."

He kissed her again, over and over, until both of them were breathless.

He drew his head back, kissed her once more, then drew his head back again.

"The gazebo?" He canted his head to the side.

She nodded her agreement.

He took her hand, and they rushed down a short pathway. It led to a cedar gazebo, octagonal in shape, a half wall bottom with screened window openings around the top. The night breeze and the scents of pine and asters wafted inside. A bench seat stretched along the walls, and Travis sat down.

He pulled her forward. She clambered up, straddling his lap. Her skirt rode up, but she couldn't have cared less. The closer she could get to him the better.

He tipped his head to kiss her. His thighs were warm against her bare legs, her knees braced on the smooth, cool, wooden bench. He looped his arms beneath her blazer, stroking her back through her thin blouse.

She shrugged out of the confining jacket and tossed it on the bench beside them. His broad hands cradled her ribcage as their kisses continued.

After long moments, she slowly straightened from him. She looked deep into his eyes, smiling with knowing anticipation. She tugged her blouse from the waistband of her skirt. Then, starting with the bottom button, she popped them free, one at a time.

His breathing was deep and even, his fingertips convulsing gently against her as he watched her progress. His gaze locked onto the seam of her blouse, eyes widening as she drew it open, revealing her lacy, white bra.

"Have I told you that you're gorgeous?" he rasped.

She slipped the blouse off her shoulders and tossed it on top of the blazer.

"You ain't seen nothing yet," she told him, reaching back to unhook her bra.

She didn't feel remotely self-conscious. She wanted him to see her. She wanted him to touch her. She wanted to make long, slow love with him tonight. Maybe she was being hotheaded and impulsive. But she couldn't bring herself to care.

She peeled off her bra, and he sucked in a tight breath.

"How did this happen?" he mumbled.

"I was born a girl."

"Thank goodness for that."

"You're overdressed," she prompted.

He lifted his gaze to hers. "Can I just sit here and stare at you?"

His words brought a smile to her lips. "For how long?"

"Forever."

"Sure," she told him, leaning down to kiss his mouth. "But we'll miss the wedding."

"What wedding?"

As she kissed him, she pushed off his jacket. It pooled on the bench behind him, and he freed his hands. She went to work on his tie, then the buttons of his shirt.

His hand closed over her breast, and she fumbled with a button, a moan escaping from her lips. His palm was warm, her breasts cold and the contrast was unbelievably arousing.

"I want you," she told him. "So very much."

"Oh, Danielle," he groaned. "I don't know how to be without you."

He ripped off his shirt, wrapping his arms tightly around her, drawing her bare breasts to his skin. He kissed her again, his mouth on hers, tongue delving.

A sense of urgency overtook her.

She got rid of the rest of her clothing and his in record-breaking time, and then, they were one.

His hands slipped up her skirt, cradling her hips, pressing her down then lifting her up, synchronizing her to the rhythm of his body. Warmth radiated from their joining. Pleasure skipped across her skin. She kissed him desperately, while her hands kneaded his shoulders, then his back, then his buttocks.

"Don't stop," she told him. "Keep going forever."

She wanted the sensation to go on and on. She was happy and safe. Travis's arms were strong around her. There was no yesterday, no tomorrow, nothing else mattered except the two of them together.

His thumbs slipped along her thighs, up to where their bodies joined. She gasped and jolted at the sensation, her head falling back and her toes curling in her shoes.

"Forever's not possible," he told her through gritted teeth.

"Now," she cried out. "Right… Now…"

He groaned his release, and her climax cascaded

through her. Her body convulsed around his, as warmth bathed her skin in pleasure.

She went limp, falling against him, her head on his shoulder, unable to move.

He anchored her close, massaging her bare skin. Then he reached for his suit jacket and draped it around her, cradling her in the warm cocoon.

When she finally found the strength to raise her head, he touched his forehead to hers.

His tone was low, almost reverent. "You rock my world, Danielle Marin."

She drew back, blinking, making a show of gazing around the gazebo. "There's still a world out there?"

His chuckle was deep. "I wish there wasn't."

She met his eyes, unfathomably beautiful. Something shimmered and bloomed inside her chest, and for a split second she feared she might tear up.

He smoothed back her hair. "Will you date me now?"

She couldn't help but smile. "I guess I'd better date you now."

"For starters, do you want to be my date at a wedding? There's a bit of family drama in the background, and a crowd of hundreds, but otherwise it should be fun."

"I would love to be your date at a wedding. I've got a really great dress."

He sobered.

So did she.

Unable to help herself, she leaned forward and kissed his mouth, gently to start. Once, twice, three times.

His hands came up, palms cradling her face. His jacket fell away, and she leaned against him, got lost in his kisses, wrapping herself around him all over again.

"What *is* this?" she gasped when they finally came up for air.

He buried his fingers in her hair. "I have no idea. But it's getting stronger."

The wedding came off beautifully, a sunny, fall day with flowers still blooming in the garden beds. Danielle loved Lisa's strapless, A-line gown, of white chiffon. It had a sweetheart neckline, and the snug bodice was accented with sparkling beads. Her blond hair was pulled back in a causal knot, held there by a jeweled comb. She carried a small bouquet of white roses and purple iris. Alex looked incredibly handsome in a black suit with a crisp, white shirt, his purple tie matching her bouquet.

Danielle had sat next to Travis in one of the front

rows, where he'd surreptitiously held her hand, stroking his thumb across her knuckles while the couple repeated their vows beneath a flower and white chiffon decorated arch.

Dinner was sumptuous and impressive. But as soon as the formality of the first waltz was complete, Travis claimed her hand and guided her onto the dance floor. A few dozen other couples joined them, and they were swallowed into the crowd.

As he drew her into his arms, Travis sighed heavily in her ear. "I've been waiting for this since you left me last night."

"It's a tough life," she gently mocked, parroting his words from yesterday.

"Tell me you missed me, too."

"I missed you, too," she admitted.

They'd said goodbye in the mansion's back foyer last night, each retiring to their respective rooms. She'd lain awake half the night thinking about him, missing his arms around her, wondering where she and Travis went from here.

"I *need* to sleep with you tonight," he told her now.

She eased back to admonish him. "Aren't you presumptuous." Even though she wanted exactly the same thing.

"No," he swiftly denied. "I mean, not that. I mean,

yes that, but only if it's what you want. What I mean is *sleep,* literally. I want you in my arms all night long." He drew her back against him. "I've realized nothing else is good enough."

As much as she'd love to spend the night in Travis's bed, she felt compelled to inject some reality into the conversation. "I don't see how we manage that."

"Not here," he agreed.

"But we are here. And so is everybody else. One of the joys of that humongous family of yours."

"A hotel," he suggested.

"Oh, that's discreet."

"We could go back to the ranch."

"Wouldn't that seem a little odd, us leaving together on a two hour drive at midnight?"

"Maybe," he allowed, going silent.

"I feel like it's prom night," she muttered.

"Backseat of my car?" he offered on a lighter tone.

"I don't think it's going to work out tonight, Travis."

They might be able to get away for an hour or so, but there was no way they could disappear for the entire night.

"It has to work out," he insisted.

"There'll be lots of other nights," she reassured him.

He drew back. "Are you serious?"

Her stomach lurched in regret, her skin prickling with embarrassment. That was entirely the wrong thing to say. What was she *thinking*? She struggled to think of a way to turn the words into a joke, dial them back.

"Will you promise me lots of other nights," he asked her. "Because I can convince myself to give this one up, but only if I know there'll be others."

"Where is this going, Travis?" she forced herself to ask him. "What exactly do you want?"

"I want to spend time with you. It's as simple and as complicated as that."

Her entire body relaxed. "I want to spend time with you too."

"That's good." He pulled her close again, kissing her surreptitiously at her hairline. "That's very, very good."

The music drew to a close.

"Travis," came Maureen's cheerful voice as she sidled up to them. "Come dance with your mom."

"Love to, Mom," he answered warmly. "Don't go far," he whispered to Danielle as she drew away.

She nodded her agreement.

Her heart singing along with the music, she all

but skipped off the dance floor. Dating Travis was complicated, but when they cut through to the heart of their attraction, it was also very simple. They liked each other, so they'd find a way.

She was thirsty, and so went in search of a bar.

The connected rooms of the mansion were crowded with guests, but the mood was joyful, and people smiled and nodded as she passed by. She was starting to recognize a few of the faces and feeling less like an outsider. She realized she was truly enjoying the evening.

A uniformed bartender greeted her as she approached one of several rollaway bars set up around the perimeter of the hall.

"Soda and lime," she requested.

"Coming right up." He deftly flipped a clean glass, filling it to the brim with ice.

While she waited, she heard Mandy's voice nearby. "Caleb hadn't even thought of it."

Danielle leaned back, craning her neck, catching a glimpse of the ice-blue, satin bridesmaid gown.

"So, it was Travis's idea?" came Katrina's voice. "Because that's sort of dangerous."

"I thought so, too," Mandy returned, as the bartender dropped a lime slice into the glass. "Caleb said that Travis was adamant he had to hire her."

The bartender filled the glass with soda water. "Here you are, ma'am." He handed it to her.

Mandy kept speaking. "Something about keeping her out of D.C."

Danielle stilled.

But Mandy wasn't finished. "She had a killer job offer there."

"What I don't get," said Katrina, "was how it's Travis's business at all. I mean, I get that he's attracted to her. But you know his track record. Why would he interfere in her career? And why would he drag Caleb into it?"

Danielle's stomach clamped down hard. She knew she had to announce herself. She had to tell the two women she could overhear. She forced herself to move back, to where she could see them.

"It's not at all like Travis," Mandy agreed. "But I think it worked out for—" Her gaze caught Danielle's, and her eyes grew huge. "Danielle," she sputtered.

Katrina whirled, her mouth forming an O of shock.

"I'm so sorry," Danielle quickly put in, hearing an edge of hysteria to her own voice. "I didn't mean to intrude. I just…" She gave a vague wave toward the bar. "I was…" She didn't know what to say. She didn't know what to do.

The only thing for certain was that Caleb had hired her as a favor to Travis. He didn't want a company lawyer. He didn't need her on his payroll. He'd been helping out a lifelong friend who wanted to sleep with her. And who'd decided he had some kind of a right to interfere in her life.

"I'm sorry," she quickly finished, turning to rush away.

"Danielle," Mandy called from behind her.

Danielle didn't look back. She plunked her full drink on the tray beside the bar and carried on through the front foyer, escaping outside to the fresh air.

She had a credit card in her handbag. She had some cash, a comb, a lipstick and a couple of tissues. It would do until she could have her other things delivered.

She trotted down the front stairs. The air was chilly against her bare arms, and through the thin dress, but that didn't matter. All that mattered right now is that she got away, away from Travis, away from Caleb, away from their families and her humiliation.

Her new job was a fraud. And she couldn't go back to the old one. She'd left Milburn and Associates on bad terms, and she'd turned down Nester and Hedley. She had absolutely no prospects. She honestly didn't know where she went from here.

A hotel first, she supposed. And then she'd need to update her resume. On the bright side—

Her breath caught and her chest tightened painfully. She couldn't seem to come up with a bright side.

The second Travis saw the expression on his sister Mandy's face, he knew something was wrong.

The song was ending, so he quickly excused himself from his mother, crossing the dance floor to meet Mandy. Katrina was hovering behind her.

"What?" He glanced from side to side, trying to identify the source of the problem.

"It's Danielle," Mandy blurted out.

Travis's stomach clenched hard. "Is she hurt?"

Mandy swiftly shook her head. "She's fine. She left."

His fear was replaced with confusion. "What? Why?"

"She overheard us. Well, me. She overheard me talking about her job at Active Equipment."

Travis still didn't understand. "She had *work* to do? Now?"

"No." Mandy drew a breath. "She heard me say you'd talked Caleb into hiring her."

Travis's world went still. Then a roaring sound started in his ears. "You didn't," he rasped.

"I'm so sorry," Mandy continued. "I think." She swallowed. "She might have heard me say you wanted to keep her out of D.C."

"Where'd she go?"

"Through the front door."

"When?" Travis demanded, his feet already moving toward the exit.

He didn't hear Mandy's answer. He elbowed his way through the colorful, laughing crowd. People spoke to him, but he didn't answer. The sounds and sights of the reception blended together, incomprehensible and meaningless. The only message that mattered was inside his head. He had to get to Danielle. He had to explain.

He burst through the big door, sprinting to the street, glancing one way and then the other.

He spotted her, half a block down, under a streetlamp, marching along in her blue dress and high heels, the crystals sparkling in the light.

"Danielle," he called.

Her shoulders stiffened, but she kept walking.

"Danielle," he repeated, breaking into a run. "Stop."

This time, there was no reaction. She completely ignored him.

His strides ate up the sidewalk, and he quickly caught her. "Danielle, please, let me explain."

She lifted her chin and increased her pace. "You don't have to explain a thing."

"Stop," he pleaded.

She stopped and turned on him. "No."

"Let me tell you what happened."

"I *know* what happened. You got Caleb to manipulate me. You couldn't keep me out of D.C. by yourself, so you made him do it for you. You are a self-centered, unbridled control freak."

"I am not a control freak, I—"

"Do you have *any* idea what you've done?" she demanded, eyes blazing under the light.

"I want what's best for you," he insisted, knowing it was entirely true.

"You don't get to decide what's best for me. Randal doesn't get to decide, and you don't get to decide."

"Randal's a selfish jerk."

She jabbed a finger against Travis's chest. "And you are exactly like him."

"I am *nothing* like him," Travis growled.

"Really?" she demanded. "He wanted to sleep with me, so he found me a job in D.C. You wanted to sleep with me, so you found me a job in Lyndon Valley. Tell me right now, what's the difference?"

The difference was that Travis wanted what was best for Danielle. Randal wanted what was best for Randal.

She didn't wait for him to answer. "The difference is, you're worse, Travis. Because you actually ruined my career. I have no job. I had two, count 'em *two* solid, viable, well-paying job opportunities, and you made me blow them both."

"You have a job at Active Equipment."

"Don't insult me. That's a sham."

Caleb's voice interrupted. "It's a real job, Danielle."

Her eyes darted past Travis to where Caleb had caught up to them on the sidewalk.

"Not you, too, Caleb," she rasped. "I trusted you. I thought we had—" Her voice broke.

Caleb stepped forward. "You *can* trust me."

"You can trust me, too," Travis felt compelled to put in. "I might have suggested—"

"Stop talking," Danielle ordered him in a stone-cold tone.

She looked at Caleb to include him as well. "Both of you stop talking. This is *my* life. You don't get to mess with it." She took a backward step away from them. "I'm leaving now."

Travis made to follow. "No."

Caleb grabbed his arm to stop him.

Travis struggled to shake off the grip. No way, no how was he letting Danielle leave like this.

"Take a car," Caleb told her, waving one of the sedans forward. "Take it to the Sunburst Hotel. Active Equipment has an account."

"I'll pay for my own hotel room," she snapped.

"Don't go," Travis barked. "Let's go someplace, let's talk."

She gazed up at him, or rather through him. "I never want to speak to you again."

The car pulled up, and she moved to the curb.

"Danielle," he pleaded, straining toward her.

Caleb's grip tightened. "Not now," he ordered in Travis's ear.

"I can't let her go."

She opened the back door of the sedan.

"You have to let her go."

As she climbed inside, Travis jerked free.

"For now," Caleb said to him. *"For now."*

Danielle slammed the door shut.

Travis swore.

"You'll talk to her tomorrow," Caleb offered.

Travis swore again.

"She'll be at the Sunburst." Caleb clasped him on the shoulder. "And you'll talk to her in the morning."

"I'm so sorry," Mandy said, surprising Travis

with her presence. "I truly did not realize she could hear me."

He wanted to rail at his sister, demand to know what had happened, demand to know how she could have been so indiscreet. But he knew it wasn't her fault. It was his fault.

He wasn't anything like Randal. But right now Danielle had no way of knowing that.

"I have to talk to her," he said out loud. He didn't think he could wait until morning.

"And say what?" asked Mandy, moving a little closer to him.

He gazed down as his practical, pragmatic sister looked him square in the eyes. "And say what, big brother?"

He didn't understand the question.

"That you're in love with her?" Mandy asked.

Something shifted inside Travis, the possibility opening up like sunshine on an early spring morning.

In love with Danielle? How great would it be to be in love with Danielle? That would mean he could care for her, protect her. He could spend the rest of his life with her. They could live together, build a family like his siblings had done. He could grow old with Danielle by his side.

"Travis?" Mandy interrupted softly.

"She hates me," he found himself saying.

"She's only angry," Mandy countered.

Travis hoped that was true. She'd been angry with him before, and he'd been able to reason with her. Maybe he could do it again this time.

"I wasn't wrong, you know," he told his sister.

"Wrong about what?"

"To keep her out of D.C. To keep her with me instead of him."

"Maybe so," Mandy allowed. "But I'm not sure that should be your opening line."

Danielle gazed at the pink glow of the sun coming up over Lyndon City. She was curled up in an armchair, facing the picture window in her hotel room, wrapped in an oversized T-shirt. Checking in last night, she'd asked about buying something to sleep in and was given the shirt out of their storage room.

It wasn't until Danielle got to her room, that she realized it was left over from the mayor's race. The shirt was roomy, long, nearly down to her knees, and emblazoned across the front it said JACOBS HAS MY VOTE. Now, she hugged it to herself, blinking away tears, pondering the irony.

She'd fallen in love with Travis last night. She thought it must have happened while they were dancing. Then again, maybe it had happened at the rehearsal, or while they were shopping. Or maybe it had happened way back in Vegas.

She didn't really know, and it didn't really matter. She was in love with Travis, and he'd betrayed her. The worst part was that he didn't even understand what he'd done. He was so stubborn, so blind, so brazenly self-confident that it never occurred to him he could make a mistake.

If Travis saw the world a certain way, then that was the way of the world. If anyone disagreed, then they were misguided. That conviction gave him license to manipulate people and events. He'd wanted her in Lyndon Valley, so here she was, in Lyndon Valley.

Yet again, her mother was proven right. Men looked after their own interests. Women were on their own.

Should she have seen this coming? Should she have guessed the depths of Caleb's loyalty to Travis?

Mentally debating what she should or should not have known, was exhausting. She knew she ought to care about her career. But all she knew at the moment was that she missed Travis. She loved him. Or at least she had loved him. For a brief magical time last night, they seemed to have a shining future.

There was an abrupt knock on her hotel room

door, and her nerves jolted to life. She gripped the arms of the chair, staying firmly in place, telling herself there wasn't anyone she wanted to see right now.

The knock came again, followed by Caleb's voice. "Danielle? I brought you some things from the mansion."

She was disappointed, and she hated herself for feeling that way. She'd wanted it to be Travis. Even in the midst of his outrageous behavior, she wanted it to be him. How could she allow herself to be so weak?

"Danielle?" Caleb called again.

She pushed herself up from the chair, gritting her teeth in determination. She would need to talk to Caleb at some point. And she did need to get her things. Better to get it over with now. Then she could make a reservation back to Chicago.

Bracing herself, she unlocked the door and pulled it open.

Her heart lurched in her chest when it was Travis standing in the hall.

They both stared at each other. He looked as exhausted as she felt.

"We need to talk," he opened softly.

She swallowed, struggling to find her voice. It was buried by heartbreak. "I don't think I can."

"Then just listen."

She shook her head in denial. "You can't do this to me, Travis."

"I want what's best for you. I always have."

A little bit of her strength returned. "You've truly convinced yourself of that, haven't you?"

"Can I come in?"

"No."

"We can't leave it like this."

"Where's your brother-in-law? Or should I say your partner in deceit?"

"He knows I need to talk to you."

"End justifies the means?" she mocked. "Yet again?"

"Let me explain. Hate me if you have to, but at least let me explain."

His beautiful, blue eyes were wide, and there was a vulnerability to his tone that wormed its way into her heart. She couldn't find it in herself to refuse.

Wordlessly, she stepped back, opening the door to him.

He immediately came in, closing the door, pressing his back against it.

For a minute, they both just stood there. His gaze flicked to her T-shirt, then to her bare legs below it. Something flared in her belly, and she hated herself for still desiring him.

"I couldn't let him have you," Travis began, his tone unguarded.

"That wasn't your choice to make."

Not that Randal had a single chance of winning her back, especially after she'd come to know Travis. Randal was nothing to her anymore.

"I was absolutely certain I was doing the right thing."

"You always are."

He nodded. "I knew you'd love working for Caleb. I knew Caleb would love having you there. It was a good fit. It was a win-win."

She found herself growing impatient. "Just admit it, Travis."

He jerked his head back. "Admit what?"

"Quit with the 'I did it for you' and 'I did it for Caleb.' Just admit you wanted to sleep with me, so you found a way to keep me around."

He pushed away from the door, taking a couple of paces into the room. "Is that what you think?"

"It's the truth."

He faced her square on. "That I wanted you around? Sure. That's the truth. But not so I could sleep with you."

"I was there, Travis, remember? I know what you wanted."

His expression softened. "Okay, yeah, I'd take you in my bed any day of the week."

Her stomach shimmered with desire again, and she fought the urge to throw herself into his arms. She wanted to kiss him. She wanted the night he'd promised her on the dance floor. Then she wanted a hundred more like it. She wanted Travis in her life every night and every day.

"I wanted you Danielle." His tone was husky. "I wanted everything about you. On some level." He coughed a harsh laugh. "I guess I already knew I was in love with you."

Her mind screeched to a halt.

"But I knew you wouldn't marry a cowboy," he continued.

Wait, what? What was that part about loving her?

"So," he told her. "I settled for the next best thing. I was wrong." He raked a hand through his hair. "I pretended I was right, because I wanted it so bad. And if you'd actually moved to D.C., I'd have had to move there too to keep an eye on Randal."

Her mind was still grappling with his declaration of love. He loved her? She wouldn't marry him? How did he know she wouldn't marry him?

"Travis—"

"I'm sorry, Danielle." He reached for her shoulders, his touch light, cradling them ever so gently.

By contrast, his tone was harsh. "But he can't have you. I can *never* let him have you."

"Travis?"

"Yes?" he choked out, faced pained, expression taut.

"You should ask me to marry you."

He blinked in obvious bafflement, his jaw going lax.

"I want you to ask me to marry you."

His expression remained taut. "Okay," he started slowly. "Will you marry me, Danielle?"

"Yes."

"What?"

"I'll marry you."

He gaped at her. "Why?"

Her lips curved into a smile. "Because I'm in love with you." She pressed her palm to his chest, covering his heart as she stepped closer. "I love you, Travis."

"I'm a cowboy."

"I know."

"You're an intelligent, accomplished, world-class legal genius."

"So we both agree, I'm smart enough to know when I'm in love?"

His arms slipped around her back. "You love me?"

She moved into his arms, resting her body against

his. "You better hope so, cowboy, since we're engaged."

"We're really engaged?"

"Unless you want to take back your proposal."

His hands moved to cradle her cheeks. "Not on your life. And you're not taking back your acceptance. We're engaged, Danielle Marin, and I'm going to marry you just as soon as we can get in front of an official. Can you be ready in an hour?"

"We're not in Vegas anymore. I don't think there's a chapel in the lobby."

"Seth will marry us. And he can expedite the license."

"You want to marry me today?"

"Yes. Absolutely. I don't want you to change your mind."

He leaned in to place a soft, lingering kiss on her lips and she basked in his gentleness and his solid strength.

"I'm not going to change my mind."

"I can't take that chance."

"Okay," she agreed on a whisper. "I'll marry you just as soon as you want."

"I love you, Danielle."

Her heart squeezed tight in her chest. "Travis, I love you so much."

He smoothed back her hair. "My family's already here. But, what about your family?"

Danielle wasn't so sure that was a good idea. "You want to argue with my mother about a prenup?"

"You want a prenup?"

"No. But she will."

He loosened his hold on her ever so slightly. "What do you want to do?"

"Elope? No frills, a simple ring, a simple ceremony. It's the outcome that matters to me, Travis, not the event."

He thought about it for a moment. "Can we tell my family before we go?"

"Sure. Maybe Katrina and Reed can come with us."

A smile grew on Travis's face. "We will need witnesses. Vegas?"

"On the deck at Jacque Alanis?"

"Katrina will make us go dancing."

"As long as you hold me close."

"I'll hold you close, Danielle," he vowed, enfolding her in his arms. "I'm going to hold you close forever."

* * * * *